Category
Five

ALSO BY ANN DÁVILA CARDINAL

Five Midnights

Category
Five

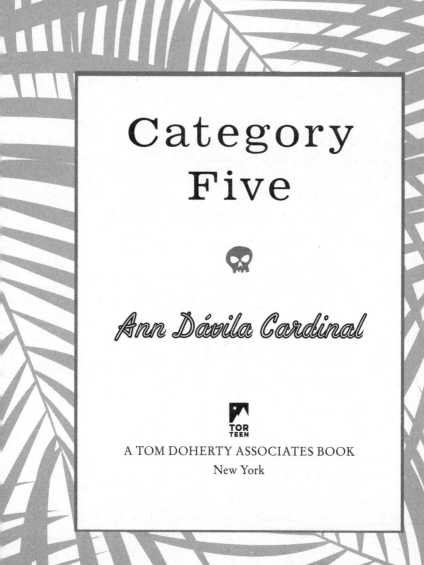

Ann Dávila Cardinal

TOR TEEN

A TOM DOHERTY ASSOCIATES BOOK

New York

CATEGORY FIVE

A Tor Teen Book
Published by Tom Doherty Associates
120 Broadway
New York, NY 10271

www.tor-forge.com

Tor® is a registered trademark of Macmillan Publishing Group, LLC.

The Library of Congress Cataloging-in-Publication Data is available upon request.

ISBN 978-1-250-29612-2 (hardcover)
ISBN 978-1-250-29613-9 (ebook)

Our books may be purchased in bulk for promotional, educational, or business use. Please contact your local bookseller or the Macmillan Corporate and Premium Sales Department at 1-800-221-7945, extension 5442, or by email at MacmillanSpecialMarkets@macmillan.com.

First Edition: 2020

Printed in the United States of America

0 9 8 7 6 5 4 3 2 1

*For my brother, George, who came up with the idea for
this book, who always supports my dreams,
and who will talk zombies with me for hours.
Te quiero, hermano.*

*And for our mother, Elena Luisa Dávila, who lived
through the 1928 category five hurricane, San Felipe II,
when it hit Puerto Rico, the stories of which haunt
me to this day.*

*And for the people of Puerto Rico, who, though it
may have seemed they were forgotten during and after
Hurricane Maria, are never far from the minds
and hearts of those who love them.*

Chapter One

Bio Bay, Vieques Island, Puerto Rico

RIGOBERTO SIGHED. ONCE again the trio of gringo college students devolved into a splashing fight, using their kayak paddles to fling arcs of glowing water at each other in the velvety dark. The miracle of bioluminescence, organisms that lit up the water like microscopic fairies, was totally lost on them. Not to mention they clearly weren't taking classes in maturity at their pretentious Ivy League university. Rigo had only just finished high school, but he was about three decades more evolved than these douchey frat boys.

He glanced over the dark bay, the stars of the moonless night reflected in the black surface of the water as if there were heavens above and below. After Hurricane Maria the mangrove trees had been practically stripped clean, but now, nine months later, though they weren't yet tall, they were proud, their roots digging deep beneath the salty water, holding strong. It would take a lot more than a category five hurricane to destroy those trees.

Not that these a-holes would appreciate the magic of the place.

He breathed deep and prepared his "guide voice."

"Gentlemen, if we could get back to the tour . . ." *so I can dump your asses downtown and head to Bananas for a cold beer and an intelligent conversation with my friends.* But he left the second half of his thought unspoken. Insulting tourists didn't go over well. He'd tried it more than once.

"Yeah, cut it out, you apes!" The leader, Jason, chastised the others with a smirk even though he was the one who had started it.

Rigoberto had met many versions of this kid during his various summer jobs on the island. They always came with an entourage, since, he figured, bullying was no fun alone. He glanced at his watch: 8:15 p.m. Only forty-five minutes more. That's all Rigo was contracted for. He could survive that long. He sat up straight and returned to tour guide mode. "The tiny island of Vieques was inhabited by indigenous peoples, the Taínos, fifteen hundred years before Columbus set foot in the Caribbean."

"Indigenous, huh?" the smallest one said, then patted his mouth and did a racist hoot, laughing. But even his Neanderthal friends seemed to recognize how offensive that was and no one laughed with him.

Actually, no. That was giving them too much credit. They just seemed to ignore everything that one said.

No one would blame me if I strangled them all and left them here. Seriously.

He twisted in his seat to look back at the group, taking a head count without even thinking. It was something you had to do when running tours. Four. He faced forward.

Wait, what?

He spun his head around and looked over the group. One, two, three. Phew! That was weird, he could have sworn he saw a fourth head. A chill passed over his skin despite the warmth of the evening. This whole trip had him on edge. To top it off, that night the bay looked . . . darker somehow. He was used to giving these tours in the pitch black since it was the best way to see the dinoflagellates light up, but there was something . . . menacing about the dark. Another shudder ran through him as he felt something brush across the back of his neck. He just needed to finish this tour so he could go back to civilization and shake this creepy vibe. He turned around and continued in a monotone voice since they weren't listening anyway, and they clearly weren't capable of actual learning. "Then, it was taken over by the Spanish, and eventually in 1941, the United States military took over two thirds of the land, displacing residents and, some say, taking advantage of the islanders when they were struggling to recover from many tragedies."

"Hey, watch it, ah-mee-go. My dad was military," Jason said.

"Of course he was." Rigoberto gave him his best and biggest patronizing smile. "So was my father, actually."

"What, like, in the Puerto Rican army?" The hairy imbecile named Steve asked.

Rigo winced. "No, the same military. You do understand that Puerto Ricans are U.S. citizens, don't you?" Okay, so *the tone* was in his voice, the tone his boss had warned him about. *They're assholes, but they come from very important families, so don't give them that superior tone of yours,* he had warned Rigoberto. But sometimes he just couldn't help it.

"Hey, I don't like your tone."

Great, now Jason was channeling his boss. He bit his tongue: he had to deescalate things. He needed this job. High school was over, and it was time to save for college. His family's restaurant had closed in the spring. Winter tourism was nonexistent since they hadn't had power and the palm trees looked like they'd been gnawed on. "I intended no disrespect, of course."

The guy grinned at him. "Of course." Then he went back to lazily running his paddle through the water.

But Rigo knew he wouldn't get off that easily.

Jason proved that by adding, "You do understand that our parents could buy this island out from under you, right?"

Don't take the bait, Rigo told himself. *Don't do it.* He kept paddling.

Jason followed with "Oh wait, we already did!" and the group dissolved into uproarious laughter and a round of fist pumping.

As he pushed his kayak through the glistening water, Rigoberto fantasized about hitting them all over the head with his paddle. "Let's continue with the tour, shall we?" Wasn't it enough that the kid Jason's father had helped buy a huge chunk of land out from under the locals to build a monstrosity of a hotel? Now he had to take this abuse? He clenched his teeth tight, the tension spidering up from his jaw into the sides of his skull.

"Why does the water glow like this again?" The one named Steve asked, as if they hadn't already gone over it several times.

Rigo took a deep breath. "As I was saying, the overly salty water of the bay is the perfect environment for the dinoflagellates, the plankton who light up the water when it's agitated—"

"Hey, like you, Steve!" The little whiny one in the last kayak interrupted.

Steve turned around. "Wattya mean?"

"Dino-flatulence! Get it?"

Steve gripped his paddle with his overly hairy hands, his knuckles whitening, and Rigo had this weird feeling things were about to get out of hand. Was Steve going to beat the kid? Was that where the dark feelings were coming from? Rigo watched him carefully—with no plan to intervene, he wasn't stupid.

But then a smile spread on Steve's face and he used his paddle to splash the other guy.

Rigoberto took a deep breath. Lord, his thoughts were dark tonight. But as the group sprayed one another, he realized this could go on all night. "Okay, okay, why don't we paddle our way across the bay to the other side where I can show you examples of red, white, and black mangroves." They moved a few yards, the only sound the dripping of water off their wooden paddles. A rustling sound came from among the greenery that ran along the shore.

"What was that?" Steve whispered, and they all froze, their heads turning nervously, staring into the darkness.

One by one they looked into each other's eyes and Rigo saw they were all scared. So, it wasn't just him. But he didn't hear anything unusual in the quiet night. "It's probably one of the stray dogs that roam the area," he whispered. The trio was silent for a few more minutes, listening as they looked around with big eyes. *Just enjoy the quiet,* Rigo thought, his heart rate slowly returning to normal. But the quiet was short-lived.

"Man, this is boring as shit." Jason threw his paddle down into the water and it hit with a blue glowing splash. Rigo watched it begin to float away and thought there was no way in hell he was going to chase that paddle down. Jason swayed in the kayak, holding his arms across his chest like a petulant toddler. A lot like a petulant toddler. He was certainly compensating for his fear the moment before. He was peacocking, chest out, bravado back in place. But Rigo could see from the dart of his eyes that he was still nervous. "Why do we have to stay in the boats? It's not like we can't swim."

"Except for Kevin," Steve added.

"I can too swim!" So, the little one's name was Kevin.

Now the toddlers were arguing. Rigo wasn't paid enough to babysit spoiled rich white kids, and he really was anxious to put the bay in the van's rearview mirror. So weird—he was usually more comfortable out here than in town. The edges of his voice got sharper with his impatience. "You can't swim here because the organisms in the water are very sensitive."

He ignored the exaggerated whispers mocking his slight accent "Ooh! Very 'sen-sa-teev'!"

"The chemicals on your bodies—deodorant, sunblock, insect repellent—kill them. We need to protect the delicate ecological balance of the system—"

Jason cut him off. "Ah, I see now. You're one of those liberal tree-hugging types. Wanna save the planet, and shit."

Don't engage, don't engage, the voice in Rigoberto's head warned. But he'd had enough, so he ignored it. "Don't you?"

"Don't I what?"

"Want to save the planet?"

"Nah, man! You can take my Hummer over my dead body!" Fist-pumping again.

"Hopefully that could be arranged." Rigo said under his breath.

Obviously not quietly enough.

"What did you say?" It was said low, but challenging, like a growl.

But Rigo's mouth didn't seem to be under his control anymore. "Actually, it's narcissistic, entitled attitudes like yours that got us in this—"

He was midsentence when Jason stood in his kayak, trying to reach for Rigo. He stood swaying back and forth as he balanced in the narrow boat was as if surprised it was on water. He seemed as if he was distracted by the movement and using it to forget about beating Rigo to a pulp. "Oh, screw you and your dino-shit!" Then he raised his arms over his head and dove headfirst into the water, the blue glow surrounding him as his arms and legs scissored beneath the surface.

Yeah, Rigo was about at the end of his patience.

"I'm afraid I'm going to have to insist we return to the van if this behavior continues." Great. Now he sounded like his third-grade teacher, Mr. Rodriguez. He hated Mr. Rodriguez. He looked around for Jason to surface.

But it was quiet. Too quiet. The water calm and glass-like. Where had Jason gone?

"Hey, do you guys see that? Those shapes under the water?" Kevin whispered as he leaned over the side of his kayak and peered into the dark water.

Rigo looked where Kevin was pointing. Did he see something, too? "It's probably just Jason," he said quietly, though he wasn't at all sure it was Jason.

Steve chuckled nervously. "You're afraid of the freaking wind blowing, Kevin!"

Kevin's voice was shrill. "No, there's two! Look! They were around here somewhe—"

A pale hand reached up from beneath the surface, the water dripping from it in black rivulets like blood. Its fingers stretched and coiled and pulled the edge of Steve's kayak over, dumping the large guy into the water in a pinwheeling mass of limbs.

Oh good, maybe something will eat him, Rigo thought, until it hit him that perhaps he was in danger, too.

Kevin screamed in a high-pitched voice, desperately paddling to turn his boat around. "See? See? I told you there were shapes in the water! Human shapes!"

Rigoberto looked at the two abandoned kayaks and began to wonder how long Jason had been under. Was it too long? Was there really something else in the water?

In that moment, two figures broke the surface and pulled Kevin into the water.

And suddenly, Rigo was sitting there alone in the middle of the bay. His heart was pounding as his kayak rocked gently from side to side. Was he next? He grabbed his paddle and, without a sound, placed it just above the water. He could make it to shore if he really booked it, then go get help.

Just then two forms breached the surface with a huge gasp of air and Rigo screamed . . . then recognized Jason and Steve as they shook the water off like large dogs, laughing and sputtering. Rigo was horrified he had actually been nervous for a second there. The splash and *thunk* of the kayak was followed by the cackling of the two other men as Kevin sputtered and shrieked to the surface, all three of them in the water now, probably killing the dinoflagellates with their negativity alone.

Rigoberto felt heat rise beneath his face.

Basta. Enough.

He efficiently turned the kayak around and started for the shore, the welcome silhouette of the van calling to him. For the first time that night, he felt good. He'd leave these assholes to get back to town themselves. He'd retrieve the kayaks in the morning. He'd catch shit from the institute's director, but it would be worth it.

He got out in the ankle-high water, yanked his kayak onto the sand, and secured it, dripping wet, onto the trailer behind the van. He climbed into the driver's seat and smiled big as he turned the key and the engine came to life. "Have a good walk back, assholes!" he yelled out the driver's side window as the van's headlights lit up the road sandwiched between dense foliage. He could still hear the sounds of roughhousing coming from the water as he pulled away. The idiots hadn't even noticed he'd left. "Serves them right." He fiddled with the radio and found a station playing reggaeton. He tapped the wheel along with the beat of Papi Gringo's latest hit, "Tormenta." Perhaps his night could be salvaged.

He was out of earshot when the screaming began.

Chapter Two

Marisol

WHEN SHE ARRIVED in Yabucoa, Marisol parked her 2001 Toyota Corolla under the only available shade, a caimito tree that was still able to protect her car from the sun even as it worked hard at pushing through the sidewalk with its tangle of roots. Not that she was worried about the paint job; no, the once-steel-gray finish had been beaten to jellyfish translucence by the Caribbean sun. It was more about the broken air-conditioning and a long-ass drive back to San Juan on Friday.

Not that it was sunny. There had been threatening dark clouds hovering on the edges of the overcast sky for days now, like actors waiting for their cue. But hadn't they had enough storms for several lifetimes? The drive along the east coast was beautiful despite the weather. You could see the scars from the hurricane, sure, but all the new growth was neon green and it made her happy to see life going on.

Life going on.

She was trying to figure out what that looked like. Life had been anything but smooth for her thus far, but after Maria . . . well, any kind of complaining felt frivolous. So, this summer she was determined to make a difference. To that end, she grabbed the petition she'd created at 2:00 a.m. that morning when she couldn't sleep. This kind of protest seemed to make the most sense until the island was back on its feet again. So many people were busy trying to meet basic needs, she wanted to help give them a voice.

Marisol took a swig from her bottle of water and walked through the center of town toward the church that had become the operations hub for all the volunteers and organizations doing repair work in the area. Pablo, an ancient man who set up his folding chair near the town's barber shop every day, waved at her and smiled his warm, toothless smile. She waved as usual and started toward the church.

No.

She stopped, convinced herself to turn around, and made her way toward him. Deep breath. "Señor, I have a petition to stop the purchasing of land by companies attempting to profit from the devastation of the hurricane." Here it comes, the ask. Best to practice on this mild old man first. "Would you be willing to sign it?" She thrust the clipboard toward him. "You'd be my first," she added, somewhat pathetically. He peered at the paper, and then looked up at her. She gave him the broadest do-gooder smile she could muster, but, truthfully, she worried it just looked like she was in pain. But he smiled back, took the proffered pen, and signed the first blank line with a shaking hand. When he gave it back to her with a nod, she let out a breath, smiled, sincerely grateful, and stepped away.

One down. She looked at the shaky scrawl on the first page, then held it to her chest in a hug. She could get used to this.

She'd been coming to this town and staying during the week since school let out for the summer, and she was getting to know the locals and the other volunteers from the island and beyond. She was usually more of a loner, an introvert who preferred a good book to human interaction, but there was something about being here for a shared purpose. And having to talk to hundreds of strangers for the petition was a perfect demonstration that she was not the same person she'd been a year ago.

But who was?

There was a nice breeze on the east coast, and she loved how she would occasionally catch the scent of flor de maga blooms riding on the air. Then it would disappear so quickly she would wonder if she'd imagined it, if it was a ghost scent of a bush destroyed by the storm. But then she would see a splash of bright red peeking out from the damaged foliage like hope. As usual, she planned to stop at the church's senior center before heading to the worksite to check in. She stepped into the dark, cool building, which had no lights on to save generator fuel and stave off the morning heat. The smell was so familiar— antiseptic, medicinal, with an undertone of urine and talcum powder. Okay, it wasn't flor de maga, but it still comforted her. For most of her childhood her great-grandmother Giga was stationed in a back room of their house, occasionally yelling out to the Virgin or her long dead husband, and Marisol would spend hours playing dolls on the old woman's chenille bedspread or applying blush and lipstick on her wrinkled, thin lips. On the island old age wasn't something you hid in a nursing home; it was right there in the next room.

"Mari!"

As her eyes adjusted to the dark interior, Marisol saw Camille, the stylish Haitian nurse who helped out with the elderly patients, walking toward her. Camille was a pro, had volunteered as a nurse in war-torn countries all over the globe, and it had taken Marisol awhile to earn the woman's trust. But sometime over the last few weeks, she'd broken through. A smile here, a hand pat there. Now, Camille pulled her in tight for a hug, the Magi's-gifts smell of her naturopath oils bringing a smile to Marisol's face. Her graying hair was cut stylish and short, and her clothes were crisp linen, practical but elegant, the mango color of the shirt a warm companion to her dark brown skin. In other words, she was a total badass.

The nurse pulled her out of the hug and held her at arm's length and then did her "staring into her soul" type thing. Did all nurses have that skill?

"Are you sleeping, Mari?"

And she was a mind reader, too. She laughed it off. "Too much to do to sleep!" Camille had no idea. Since the nightmares of the previous year had faded, she slept so much better. Just probably not long enough.

Camille did that cheek-pinching thing older women tended to do with teenagers. The woman's skinny strong fingers had a pincer-type feel. But it also felt like family.

"You have to take better care of yourself, niña! Don't make me drive out to Isla Verde and force chamomile tea on you!"

Family always includes just a dash of guilt and reprimand.

"I'm fine, Camille! Worry about your patients, not me."

Her lips pulled into a reluctant smile. "Someone has to take care of you. You're too busy taking care of everyone else!"

"Look who's talking."

Camille did that dismissive wave thing again.

"How's Abuelita today?"

Camille turned to look at the tiny old lady in the wheelchair nodding off in the corner, her frail body wrapped in a thick cotton blanket despite the heat. Her real name was Ofelia Gutiérrez, but everyone just called her "Abuelita" because she was like everyone's grandmother.

"Ay bendito, bless her, she's doing well today, gracias a Dios. I think she'll enjoy a visit from you." Camille glided off to reprimand one of her charges for shuffling toward the exit in his old-man slippers. Every hour or so he would insist he was going to walk back to Rincón, the town on the far west coast of the island that he came from, and she would convince him to wait until after lunch, or a nap, or dinner.

Marisol pulled a folding chair next to Abuelita and took her cool, dry hand with its papery skin into hers. The woman didn't move, her chin on her chest, rising slightly with every breath. Mari's phone dinged with a text. She pulled it out with her free hand.

Hey! I'm here! Heading 2 Vieques w/ Tio. When can I c u?

"Vieques?" Marisol said out loud, smiling at the message from Lupe. She was so glad her friend was there for the summer, but why was she going straight to Vieques? At least it wasn't far from Yabucoa.

"Vieques?" Abuelita echoed. She tended to repeat pieces of conversation that happened around her like a gray-haired parrot.

"Hola, Abuelita! Es Marisol. ¿Como se encuentra?"

"My grandmother is in Vieques. She's . . ." She appeared to lose her train of thought. Another frequent occurrence.

Marisol smiled. Abuelita was eighty-eight. She doubted her grandmother was in Vieques or anywhere at this point. Besides, Abuelita was from St. Croix, not Vieques. But Marisol hated how most people talked to the elderly as if they were children, so she always responded to their questions and comments, no patting of hand and patronizing, *Sure, honey, whatever you say.*

"Why would your abuela be in Vieques?"

Abuelita didn't seem to hear; she was nodding her head up and down in that way she did when she was lost in her own thoughts. Marisol decided she would sit with her for a few more minutes, then head over to the worksite. She was already focusing on what lay ahead on the repairs to the Vazquez's house when Abuelita spoke again.

"She's angry."

"Who? Your abuela?"

"Yes. She's so angry. . . ."

"At you? No, Abuelita, who could be angry at you?" She stroked the woman's thinning hair, trying to comfort her. Mari often wondered where the woman's thoughts went, or when. She would have to do some research into cognitive functions of the elderly.

"Not at me, at them. They made us leave . . . left her there alone," Abuelita said again, then looked up at Marisol with tears welling in her cloudy eyes.

"Oh no! Don't cry! It's okay!" Marisol's throat tightened and she thought she would cry too. How had she upset the woman?

And then Camille was there, all comforting hushes, and lifted Abuelita to her feet gently, as if she were a bird, and walked her over to her room. Abuelita was snoring before the nurse had finished tucking in the white blankets.

Then Camille came back and looked over at Marisol and noticed the tears in her eyes. "Oh no, sweetheart, it's nothing you said! The old ones, they get sad sometimes. So much loss . . ."

"She was talking about her grandmother being angry. And on Vieques. Isn't she from St. Croix?" Camille handed her a tissue and she blew her nose.

"She is, but maybe she had family from there. Don't worry, amor, she's just confused."

Marisol shivered, though the room was quite warm. No wonder the poor old woman was anxious. She'd lost her home to a hurricane. Marisol swallowed so she wouldn't start crying again. She hugged Camille and left quickly, anxious to get to work.

The last ten months had been like something from a post-apocalyptic nightmare. Volunteering was something, but Marisol had to do more. She looked at the clipboard in her hand and considered tossing it in the car but decided she would bring it to the worksite and gather some more names. But what good was the petition if she couldn't get it to the right people? The people in power.

Marisol vowed right then that she would do whatever it took to help get the island past this, whatever she could do to help people like Abuelita recover from Maria.

She just didn't know how yet.

Chapter Three

Lupe

💀

"LUPE, WOULDN'T YOU rather spend the day on a beach on the mainland? Luquillo Beach is only a twenty-minute drive from the ferry terminal. I can pick you up on the way home this afternoon. There is no need—" Esteban's voice was raised so he could be heard over the chugging of the ferry's weary engines.

Lupe smiled up at her uncle standing beside her, his thick, hairy forearms resting on the deck's railing. "Don't even bother to finish that sentence, Tío. You know damn well"— she smiled at his head-snap at the profanity—"*darn* well that I'd rather hang with you while you do your badass job than lay on a bunch of microscopic rocks and shells baking like a pale scone."

Esteban sighed. He did that a lot when they were together. At this point she felt it was her duty to exasperate him. She had noticed a spreading of gray across his hair on either side of his rugged face, even a sprinkling in his thick mustache, but the white only brought out the warm olive tan of his skin. So she was aging him. At least he was aging well.

"I don't understand why you insist on talking like one of my street informants. And I do not have a clue what a 'scone' is."

"Pastry, triangle-shaped, dry. Tastes like sawdust pressed together. You'd probably like it. It's old-people food."

He glared at her as a smile snaked up the edge of his lips.

Their relationship had settled into this after the "Cuco Event," as she liked to call it: a light layer of teasing banter covering a fierce loyalty and unconditional love.

Vanquishing a supernatural demon together bonds people, don't you know.

At least with Esteban. Her boyfriend, Javier, was a different story these days. But that's why she'd insisted on coming along on this little trip right after landing in San Juan. Javier was working in Vieques.

They stood in silence for a few minutes and Lupe enjoyed the feeling of the saltwater spray on her face. She'd been looking forward to coming down to Puerto Rico and spending the summer with her uncle and aunt all winter and spring long. Since her father had been working on his sobriety, life in their small Vermont town had been getting better, but there was something about coming to the island and her uncle's house that felt like . . . coming home. She needed to have that sensation beneath her feet, like the world was where it should be. Her uncle was the originator of that feeling in her. She had nightmares about him and her aunt moving away from the island, leaving her like a raft unmoored from shore.

She shook off a chill and changed the subject. "Why have I never heard of Vieques?"

Her uncle shrugged. "It's difficult to get there, and most Puerto Ricans go to Culebra, the island next door." He pointed to a strip of land topped by a head of palms, still recovering from the hurricane, with their tall, stripped stalks and bright green lollipop tops.

"Why?"

"Once the U.S. military took over Vieques much of it was not available to civilians."

"That doesn't sound fair."

"Well, they're gone now."

Lupe had read quite a bit about it on the way from the airport when she'd found out they were going straight there. The island had been taken over by the Scottish—for, like, a day—then Denmark, then by Brandenburg-Prussia, wherever that was. The island seemed to have been caught in a game of keep-away for most of its history.

Lupe could kind of understand how it must feel, having spent much of her life being shuttled between Vermont and her father's family in Puerto Rico. Javier was another reason she had started to feel at home on the island. But a few months ago, after the hurricane, he started to act slightly distant, and seemed impatient to get off their chats. He insisted there was nothing wrong, that it was just the nightmare after Maria, but she knew she was not imagining his distance.

She would bet her life on it.

Vieques was growing bigger as they approached, and she could see the whirling blue lights of squad cars waiting near the dock. "What's the case?" That's the kind of question that used to get her shut down, but not anymore. As Esteban had often reminded her in the last year, she had a natural gift for detective work and was more helpful to him than half of his own officers.

"Dead tourists in the bio bay. Three college students from a boat tour."

Damn. Lupe loved bio bays. Javier had taken her to the one in Fajardo at the end of last summer. The water lighting up as the kayaks sliced through had been like a religious experience. Blue glowing halos all around. But dead bodies kind of took the magic out of it. "I take it sharks are out of the question since you're getting involved?"

"Nope, not sharks. They don't like shallow waters anyway."

An officer approached them, smiled at Lupe, and looked at her uncle with the manner of a dog afraid he would be hit. Lupe chuckled. She loved how everyone was so afraid of the big, powerful man, when to her he was a total softy.

The ferry staff scuttled around on the lower decks, preparing to dock on the rapidly approaching port, and her uncle was pulled away.

Lupe closed her eyes and relished the solitude. Preparing for the trip down here at the end of the school year had been crazed. Junior year finals, early college applications, Alateen meetings. But it was worth it so she could be in the same room with Javier for the first time since last summer. Hell, the same country. His fall semester at the University of Puerto Rico ended before it began, thanks to the hurricane, and he had to skip the spring semester to save money to live on. The poor guy never got a break. No wonder he had been so gloomy lately. She had to try to give him more space.

The boat pulled alongside the dock with a long, painful scrape that sounded like a dental drill.

"Lupe, ¡ven acá!" Esteban called from below. The minute she joined him on the lower deck, they were hustled into a waiting police car.

The squad car bumped over the rutted dirt roads that led away from Isabel Segunda, the unofficial capital of Vieques. The small town reminded her of rural Vermont. Quaint, colorful buildings, lots of greenery, but worn around the edges.

They hadn't gone far before the houses started getting scarce and the road even bumpier, if that was possible. Where were they going? She leaned forward to talk to her uncle through the window that divided the front seat from back in the cruiser. "Where is the hotel that Javier is working at?"

"I thought you were the grammar queen?" Esteban gave her a sideways smile.

"Pray tell, esteemed Uncle, where is the hotel at which Javier is working?"

"That's better. It is in Puerto Diablo."

Lupe got that tight feeling in her stomach. Been awhile since she'd had that. About a year, in fact. "Um, Devil's Port?"

"Yes. The Spanish invaders thought the bio bay was lit by evil gods." Esteban snorted.

Lupe didn't find it as funny.

She fell back in her seat. "Great." She watched the unending greenery rush by the windows as the radio squawked, and her uncle and the local officer chatted in Spanish. It was as if they were driving through a tunnel of foliage, the walls a mosaic of every green imaginable, the sun filtering through like lace. She had expected the post-hurricane island to look . . . well, barren. Some of it had on the drive to Ceiba, but here in the heart of nature it was as if nothing had touched it, or even could. She put her face up to the open window and took a long, deep breath, the scent of earth, salt, and growing things reaching in and, as she exhaled, emptying her crowded brain.

The car jolted as if hitting turbulence and Lupe's head banged against the top of the window frame. She rubbed her head with one hand and held on to the overhead grab bar with the other. "Um, you'd think if they're building a fancy resort, they would make the road a bit smoother."

The officer answered. "This area was only accessible by boat up until last month, Miss. They are going to make it smoother before it opens."

"Why weren't there roads leading to it before?"

He shrugged.

She hated that kind of answer. It wasn't an answer.

Her uncle offered, "After Hurricane Maria big investors started buying up property."

Lupe sneered. "The vultures descend."

The officer nodded his head. "Well, people were unhappy about the building on this part of the island—it is right up against the wildlife refuge. But this resort will provide many jobs. It already has."

"Yeah, but at what cost?"

The silence in the car was enough of an answer for her.

The greenery on either side of the road ended abruptly, and they drove into a clearing the size of a football field. Workers hustled like bees around a massive hive of white cinder-block buildings. The car made its way around a large round fountain, the intricately tiled bowl empty of water, but gathering sand at its edges. They pulled up under the entrance portico, the workers stopping to watch as Esteban and Lupe got out. She was slowly getting used to the attention involved in being the niece of Puerto Rico's chief of police, but it was still kind of weird.

"Okay, let's find Javier," her uncle declared, about to stride off on his long legs.

She grabbed him by the arm. "No, Tío, please! I can find him myself." Ugh. Talk about humiliation. She didn't need an escort: she was practically seventeen! "Why don't you go on to the crime scene? I'll join you soon."

He looked down at her with that piercing glare of his.

She threw up her hands. "C'mon, seriously? It's midday, and there's, like, a thousand people around here." She gestured at the workers around them.

"How will you get there to meet me?"

"Javier can drive me. Or I can walk."

"No. Absolutamente no." His voice had that "open up, it's

the police" tone, the one that made people jump. Well, people other than her.

Lupe rolled her eyes. "Okay fine, I'll get a ride. I can handle myself, Tío!"

The radio squawked and she could hear a voice asking about the chief's ETA. And his cell phone chirped. She could always count on the pull of his job at times like this.

He sighed. "Very well." He pointed a finger in her face, and, in their time-honored ritual, she made to bite it. "But you call me if you need a ride. I can have one of my officers come—"

"Yes, Tío, whatever you say, Tío, of course—"

"Basta! Enough of your sarcasm." He opened his phone, barked into it as he folded his tall frame into the passenger seat, and waved as the car pulled away. The original multitasker.

With a flip phone.

Gotta love old people.

Lupe took a deep breath. She loved her uncle like crazy, but she was just not used to his patriarchal ways. Her father had sobered up in the last year, but he still let her do whatever she wanted. He'd kind of lost the right to parent when she'd had to take care of his drunken grumpy ass for most of her life.

She pulled out her own cell phone but, unlike her uncle's, her smartphone didn't seem to have any service in this part of the island. So much for texting Javier. He'd said something in their last chat about laying stones on a patio, so she started to walk around the building to find something that looked like a patio with a handsome teenage boy.

Her heart raced at the idea of seeing him again in person, finally. It was too bad he had to work all summer, but maybe she could talk her uncle into bringing her out here more often during the week. But minus the dead bodies next time.

But then, there always seemed to be dead bodies involved. What was up with that?

As she walked around to the back corner of what appeared to be the main building, she looked up and stopped short. The vista that spread out before her literally took her breath away. A half carpet of transplanted and overly perfect grass led up to a sugar-sand beach and a huge expanse of crystal-clear turquoise water, its gentle waves glistening at the crests like they were topped in diamonds. She'd been coming to Puerto Rico every summer of her life and she'd seen beautiful spots, but never anything like this. It was totally untouched. That is, if you ignored the pounding of hammers and whine of saws in the background.

"It's beautiful, isn't it?"

Lupe jumped; she'd been so lost in the view she hadn't noticed the boy who had come up beside her. She looked over and saw that he was blond and blue-eyed, tanned but in that "I have leisure time to spend at the Hamptons" entitled white guy kind of way. To top it off, he had donned a clichéd ensemble: tennis whites. Christ, did anyone even wear tennis whites anymore? Especially people who appeared to be not all that much older than her? When he smiled with his bright white and perfectly shaped teeth, she realized he looked like he'd walked off a page of a magazine.

"Yeah, it sure is." She examined him with a look that she realized was probably just like her uncle's. "Um, this place isn't really set up for tourists yet, is it?"

His eyes crinkled in question, then he smiled, realizing she meant him. "Is it that obvious I'm not local?"

"You might say that." Lord, he even held himself in an entitled way, his shoulders back, his head tossing here and there.

"Ah, but you haven't seen me salsa yet." He put one hand flat against his stomach and the other up in the classic salsa pose and began to shuffle around in a not-totally-shabby salsa step. *Very white boy* could move his hips.

She couldn't help it, she chuckled.

"Besides, who are you to talk?"

Just a bit of her guard went up. "What do you mean?"

"Well, you sure look like a tourist."

The heat flamed behind her eyes, and she was about to rip him a new one when she heard her name.

"Lupe?"

And then Javier was walking up to her in all his brown-eyed glory, his dark curls held at bay under a faded baseball cap. As she expected, he had gotten even more handsome. The outside work had warmed his skin to a golden brown, and highlights of copper glistened in his hair. He might well have attained godlike status since she'd seen him last. He stepped close and went to hug her, his gaze grabbing hers in that way that made her skin feel hot and shivery all at once. But then he noticed tennis-whites guy and stopped.

Javier looked over at him with a smile that was tight in a way probably only she would notice. He nodded at the boy. "Sam."

And Sam Tennis Whites nodded back, his smile also slightly tight. "Javier."

Lupe just grinned. Oh, she was *totally* going to have to get the scoop on this playground tension. Boys were such a trip.

Sam put his hands up as if in a truce. "Well, guess I better go. Nice to meet you—" He waited for her name like someone who got an answer to every question.

Lupe never had been the kind of person who obliged people like that. She just kept smiling and nodded. "Yeah, nice to meet you too, Sam."

He paused for a second, his toothpaste-ad smile wider when he realized she hadn't given him her name, and then walked away, hands in the pockets of his tiny white shorts.

"What a pendejo," Javier said under his breath.

Lupe's cousin taught her all the necessary swear words, so even she knew what that meant. "Who is that guy?"

"Nobody of importance. He's the developer's son."

"Developer?"

"The man who bought this part of the island and is building the resort."

"Ahh, I see." Now Lupe understood the slight sneer on Javier's lips, the distaste he had for this Sam guy. Javier took her hand and started walking toward the trees. "C'mon, it's too public here, I feel like we're in a fishbowl."

As she followed, she looked back at the expanse of tropical-calendar beach. "Yes, but what a fishbowl."

They walked through a break in the trees and over a path of long gray marble stones. She looked up and into the deepening jungle, and asked, "What are these stones here for? The lagartos?" She imagined a line of the bright green lizards marching up and down the marble.

"They lead to a storage building." He pointed to a large concrete box on the left, no windows, just double red doors.

"Is that where you're bringing me? How romantic!" But then he was pulling her to him, kissing her hard, as if trying to combine all the kisses they'd missed after being separated those long months. Lupe pulled off his baseball cap and threw it to the side, digging her fingers into his thick, dark curls. His tongue slipped in and out of her mouth as if searching for something. When they separated, she had to catch her breath, the whole island spinning as she stared into his deep brown eyes. "Well, it is pretty damn romantic after all."

He answered with a soft, slow kiss, their lips sticking slightly as they separated as if wanting to hang on longer. "God, I missed you, Lupe."

She ran her fingers over his sharp cheekbones. They'd gotten sharper since she'd last seen him. "I missed you too, Javi."

Looking into his eyes, she said, "I'm sorry about all you've been through; sorry I couldn't be here with you."

"No, I'm glad you weren't here! I felt better knowing you were safe."

She smiled. "You sound like my uncle."

Javier didn't let go of her, but he looked away. "I don't know what I would have done without your uncle through all that. Taking me and my mom in like that? He's, like, a saint or something."

She laughed, "He thinks so, anyway." But then she got serious, taking his face in her hands. "That's what we do for people we love." And then she kissed him, wrapping her arms around his neck, pulling him as close as she could.

Lupe wished they could stay there, standing with their bodies pressed against each other, leaves and branches and wildlife rustling all around them. The way he looked at her, like he wanted to crawl inside and inhabit the same space, made her knees shake. She'd dreamed of this moment for months and months. Forever, it felt like. But then in the distance, back toward the resort, someone dropped something big, the sound echoing through the clearing, and reality was back.

Damn reality.

He pulled his body away, slowly, reluctantly, took her hand, and they started to walk back to the worksite.

"When can I see you?"

She smiled. "You're seeing me now."

He lifted her hand to his mouth and kissed her knuckles, his lips soft and gentle. A feeling traveled along her skin like electricity.

"I need to see you alone."

There it was, the island was spinning again.

He stopped, held on to her upper arms, and looked at her from the top of her head to the turquoise of her fresh pedicure, in that way he had where she felt his gaze like heat. "I'm so happy you're here." He carefully put his fingers under her chin and leaned in, his lips gently pressing against hers, his smell of warmth and salt and boy sweat making her head swim.

He pulled away and looked around.

She felt the blush at her hairline when it hit her. "Oh right. You're at work."

He smiled at her with that one-side-higher-than-the-other grin she'd grown to know so well and she had to shake her head to clear the fog Javier tended to put her in. Maybe she just imagined there was something wrong.

"I have to get back to work."

"Right." She hated that he had to work all summer, but he needed money to live on while he went to college in the fall and she supported his wanting to pay his own way.

He took her hand again and started walking back toward the hotel's main building as the percussion of construction came back into focus. When she was with him it really was as if everything else faded away. She wasn't sure that was entirely good, but it sure felt good.

"Do you need a ride to meet your tío?"

Lupe was about to answer when a car engine roared in the small partially finished parking lot up ahead. She didn't know about cars, but even she could tell this was a nice one. Convertible, white and shiny, rounded lines like a cat stretching. And then she noticed Sam's blond head above the steering wheel, his eyes masked by large, dark sunglasses.

"No, I can get a ride," she said absently, distracted by the ridiculous shininess of the boy and his car. Lupe realized Javier was staring at her and she looked up at him. He was giving her the look. "What?"

"Stay away from him, Lupe."

"What? Who?" She really was confused, mainly because

she'd never seen his face like this, the lines on either side of his mouth like angry slashes.

He tossed his head in the direction of the car. "Sam. Stay away from him."

Then it finally hit her what he was saying. She dropped his hands and put hers on her hips. "Excuse me?"

The flame in her own eyes must have flared because then he tried to backpedal. "He's not to be trusted. He thinks because his father is the owner, he can do what he wants—"

"Uh-uh, Javier, I was talking about getting a ride from one of my uncle's officers, but more to the point, you don't get to tell me who I can and can't hang out with." She didn't know this guy Sam and couldn't care less about him, but she was damned if she was going to tell Javier that now.

"What, you like him?" He started waving his arms like he was directing traffic or something. "Of course you do, he's rich and flashy—"

What was wrong with him? "Oh no, you clearly have learned nothing about me in the last year if you think either of those things mean shit to me."

"How do I know what you've been doing for the past year? We've been in two different worlds." He was pacing now like a caged tiger.

"I don't know, maybe because we FaceTimed every freaking night?" He was really pissing her off now. Hadn't they just been kissing in the trees? How had this gotten so out of control?

"It's just . . . Lupe, that guy is yet another colonizer taking this island for all it's worth!"

"What? He's, like, eighteen years old! He's not colonizing shit!"

He scoffed. "You just don't get it."

"I know I don't, but focusing your anger on that kid is a

waste of time. I don't care for this big, ugly McResort either, but there are more effective ways to fight this, to find an outlet for all this understandable anger. Marisol is—"

He put up his hand. "I know what Marisol is doing." He looked like he was about to say something else, but seemed to change his mind. "Bueno, forget it." He grabbed her hand again, but not in the gentle laid-back way he normally did, and started pulling her toward the front of the property.

Lupe pulled her hand free, a heat beginning to rage in her chest, behind her face. Ever since September it was as if a piece of the hurricane had parked itself around Javier's head, the storm raging and thrashing behind his dark eyes. "Look, I understand you're pissed, but don't be trying to drag me around like your pet poodle." She started marching away, thoughts sparking in her head like lightning. The tears that were threatening only made her angrier. What had she done to deserve being treated like this? Nothing, that's what. But that didn't make her feel any better. As she walked, she was aware of every stone that skittered away at the thump of each step over the sparkling new gravel.

"Lupe! Wait!"

She stalked by a pair of men balancing a flowering tree, roots and all, over a neat hole in the ground. They froze as she passed, tree still in hand, probably stunned by the electricity shooting off her skin. She should have stayed in Vermont. No. She loved it on the island, loved seeing her aunt and uncle and her best friend Marisol. She would not let Javier's cranky ass take that away from her.

When she reached the beginning of the empty road that led away from the resort, the tears finally broke free, and she felt them run down her hot cheeks. How could she have been so wrong about him? She walked with her head down and wondered if she could take an earlier ferry and wait for her uncle at the other side, in Ceiba. She had to at least get off this island and back to the main island. She wanted water between her and Javier. She couldn't think straight.

Lupe became aware of a vehicle coming up behind her, and she moved closer to the trees on the side of the road. Hopefully they'd just pass on by.

No such luck. A beat-up blue truck with a landscaper's logo on the door pulled up beside her and slowed.

"Lupe, I'm sorry."

At the sound of Javier's voice her heart and her feet started moving faster.

The truck kept pace with her. Javier put his arm along the back of the passenger seat, leaning over toward the open window. "Lupe, please get in. I'm sorry."

No. She would not be swayed by the softening of his voice, by the way his eyes were lit by the sun peeking into the truck.

"Listen, three guys were murdered here yesterday. It's not safe—"

"Oh, I've faced worse," she snapped.

Javier nodded. "Yes, I know you—"

She stopped and crossed her arms. "No, clearly you don't!" She waved back toward the parking lot. "What the hell was that back there about Sam? I don't even know that guy!"

Javier pulled his arm back and slumped in his seat, his body deflating like the air had been let out. "I know," he said finally. "It's me, not you. I'm just not the same since Maria. It's like that storm . . . it chewed us up and spat us out."

The truck slowed and Lupe found herself slowing with it, listening. There had been those few terrible days when she couldn't reach him, when she imagined the worst. Later, when she asked him about it, he didn't want to talk. She learned more from her uncle, and he used words like they were being rationed.

"El Cuco . . . I thought that was the worst thing that would ever happen to me. I thought if I could survive that, I could survive anything." He stopped the truck and stared straight ahead.

The air slowly released from Lupe's anger like a long-held breath. Silently, she opened the passenger door and slid into the seat.

He started driving, slowly, talking as he looked straight ahead. "I don't like feeling so angry. It's just, this is the only work I could get this summer." He gestured back at the hotel as if it were listening. "I hate working for these vultures."

"The developers?"

He nodded, his mouth a straight line, his eyes still in the distance. He looked over at her. "What kind of people take advantage of a natural disaster? To make money?"

Lupe looked right back at him. "Monsters."

Monsters were something they both knew a lot about.

Chapter Four

Javier

💀

JAVIER DROVE SLOWLY, trying to drag out the time with Lupe despite the strained silence between them. Their reunion had started out so well. He'd tried to hold back, to play it cool, but holding her, kissing her after all these months had been so good. Then he'd screwed it up.

Sam. What an asshole. For a month Javier had seen him parading around, flaunting his wealth and his overpriced sports car. But truth was, he was only really pissed at himself. His thoughts were so dark these days, since Maria, that it took every ounce of energy he had to stay clean and sober. He worked, went to Narcotics Anonymous meetings, and dropped into bed at the end of the day. This routine was the only way to quell the storm inside of him. It was like the hurricane never left, like it was still raging inside his skull, the sharp edges of debris smashing against the sides. His priest mentor, Father Sebastian, told him it was like Javier was boxing against a shadow on a brick wall: the only person left hurt and bleeding was him.

He snuck a glance at Lupe beside him, the bright sun lighting her just at the knees, her pale skin beneath her shorts shimmering like a pearl. She looked over, catching him gaping at her legs, and he snapped his head back to the front.

God, she scrambled his brains.

He hoped that looking wasn't all she'd let him do after the way he'd acted. The absolute last thing you do with Lupe is try to control her, he knew that better than anyone.

"Idiota," he snarled to himself.

"Did you say something?" Lupe asked.

He shook his head. His phone ringing jolted him from the console. He didn't have to look at it to know who it was: Carlos. His friend had changed the ringtone on Javier's phone to one of his own Papi Gringo hits. Classic.

"Aren't you going to get that?"

"Huh?"

"The phone. It's Carlos, isn't it?"

"Nah, I'll catch him later." Truth was, he'd been calling several times a day all week, but Javier just did not have the patience to talk to him. Probably some television host asked a difficult question, or they didn't have the right color M&M's in his dressing room. Nah, he wasn't like that, but having a best friend who was a celebrity was not nearly as entertaining as everyone thought it was. Besides, there were so many real-life horrible things going on for the island, for their people right now, how could he deal with Carlos's celebrity life?

They came up on a line of police cars up and down the road ahead.

"Your uncle is never hard to find." He snorted.

Lupe wasn't laughing. Worse, she was gathering her stuff and getting ready to get out of the truck.

Say something! he chided himself.

"Lupe, I—"

"Javier—"

They both laughed. When had they ever *not* been comfortable around each other?

Someone appeared at the driver's side window and Javier leapt in his seat, squealing a bit like his tía's ancient chihuahua. He grabbed his chest when he saw the mustached, intense face of Lupe's uncle.

"You afraid, Utierre?" A small smile was on the big man's face.

"No, Chief Dávila, you just startled—"

"Yeah, well, lots to be startled about around here." He gestured toward Lupe, who had just slid off the bench seat of the truck and dropped to the dirt road with a little hop. "Lupe, come with me." He pulled away from the window, and Javier breathed out.

But then the chief stuck his head back in the window and Javier jumped again.

"On second thought, come with us, Utierre. I want to talk to you too." And then he was gone again.

Javier looked over at Lupe and she shrugged.

They fell into step behind the tall man, and Javier was very aware of Lupe's hand swinging inches from his, but he was going to have to warm things up before he dared take her hand again. And certainly not in front of her uncle.

Esteban Dávila stopped along a stretch of rocky shore. Javier glanced over and saw a group of uniformed EMTs carrying off three stretchers, each with a zipped body bag balanced on top. He swallowed hard. He knew that the bags contained three guys, not much older than he and Lupe. Javier had lost three lifelong friends the previous year to addiction . . . and El Cuco, the monster called forth from childhood nightmares.

"Utierre." The commanding voice called him back from his bout of déjà vu.

Lupe and her uncle were standing near the edge of the water, away from other people.

But Javier's attention was still on the bodies. "What happened to them?" he asked quietly, gesturing to the stretchers now being loaded in ambulances that idled by the side of the road.

"Someone cut their hearts out."

Javier and Lupe jolted as if the words were a blow. They actually were. Javier appreciated that after all they'd been through the previous year, the chief was so straight with them, but damn.

Lupe cleared her throat. "I take it you don't mean that metaphorically?"

Dávila just shook his head. Then he pulled the two in even closer. "Some of the people, even some of the police, for God's sake, are whispering that El Cuco has come back."

Javier's heart started pounding behind his eyes. "What?"

Lupe put her hands on her hips. "Wait, I thought they didn't buy the supernatural explanation for last year, and blamed you for leaving it unsolved?"

Her uncle nodded. "Some do, but others . . . That's why I wanted you both here."

Lupe nudged Javier and gestured toward a small group of rescue personnel who were staring at them, whispering among themselves. After the "incident" last summer, he experienced this kind of attention often, eyes following him, whispers as passersby recognized him. Sometimes someone would be bold enough to come up to him and ask, "Are you the guy who fought El Cuco at the Papi Gringo concert?" Yeah, it had been pretty much the most exciting event in the last decade.

But then the hurricane hit.

Maria.

Then El Cuco paled in comparison and Javier was left in

welcome anonymity again. Until, it seems, now. "Who were they? The boys who were killed?" Perhaps there was a clue there.

"They were all sons of investors in the resort."

Lupe and Javier looked at each other. "You mean the one Javier works for?"

"Yes. Their parents dumped them here for spring break and took off for the Maldives. From the boys' records, you can tell that happened often. Grand larceny, felony vandalism, sexual assault. Expensive lawyers come in and all charges are magically dismissed, victims refuse to press charges, you get the picture."

"So, you're saying they really are candidates for El Cuco," Lupe asked, chewing on her lower lip.

El Cuco was . . . *is* the Latin equivalent of the boogeyman. When parents want their kids to behave, they say, "You best behave or El Cuco is going to get you!" Well, last year Javier found out he was more than a myth. All three of his friends who were killed were addicts, drug dealers, basically ill-behaved under any definition.

"Holy shit!" Lupe exclaimed, and her uncle shushed her.

He was the only one on the planet who could get away with shushing Lupe.

She lowered her voice. "You said these guys were college students, right? Like, starting their second year this fall?"

"Right. One of them would have started his third, but I don't think even his rich father could buy him out of those grades."

"So, they're over eighteen, right?"

Esteban and Javier looked at each other and a smile of relief spread over each of their faces. "Right!" They said simultaneously. They had established that last year's murders occurred on the eve of the victims' eighteenth birthdays, because once they turned eighteen, they were no longer children and El Cuco would no longer have any power over them. So, if the boys were over eighteen, it couldn't be El Cuco.

But the chief added, "Then the question remains, who did kill them? We won't get people to let go of the El Cuco explanation unless we find the actual killer."

Something about this wasn't making sense to Javier. "Why do people think something supernatural killed them and not just a serial killer or something?"

Dávila took off his hat and wiped his face in a downward motion. "Yeah, that."

Lupe looked at her uncle through narrowed eyes. "There's something you're not telling us, Tío, isn't there?"

"I know what you're thinking, Lupe, and it's not to protect you. It's just it . . . seems so silly."

"Sillier than the boogeyman killing kids because they don't behave?"

He froze for a second, then said, "Point taken, sobrina. Okay, it seems that people in the villages of Esperanza and Isabel Segunda saw . . . beings last night."

Javier grew confused. "Like human beings?"

"Like dead human beings."

Lupe gasped. "Zombies? They're real? I knew it!"

She loved *The Walking Dead,* and any ridiculous undead movie, but she couldn't be happy about this . . . could she? But zombies weren't what had first come to Javier's mind. "Or ghosts?"

"Heart-eating ghosts?" She put her hands on her hips in classic Lupe fashion. "I don't think so."

The chief held out his hand in the stop gesture, as if that could slow his niece's roll. "Now let's not get out of hand. We don't know if the killer actually . . . *ate* the hearts. They're just . . . *gone.*"

"What, so they stole them? To do what with? Decorate their ghostly living rooms?"

Lupe did seem to be enjoying this, but Javier's lunch was pushing against his gullet. Why was this darkness always around him? Was it following him? Or did he bring it out? *It's not always about you*, he reminded himself.

"I'm less concerned with *why* right now than I am with *who*. Or *what*," he added as an afterthought. Lupe's uncle had not been a supernatural-believing kind of man before last summer. But they'd all had to open their minds to the possibilities.

They stood in silence for a moment, that last word hanging in the air, until the roar of engines and sounds of shouting carried over from the other entrance to the bay. Vans with news station logos on the sides squealed to a stop, disgorging overly made-up people in cheap suits, and the police chief sighed.

"Shit."

Lupe gaped at her uncle. "Language, Tío!"

The chief threw his hands up. "Then you go talk to them!"

Lupe smiled. "No, thanks. I'd rather have a root canal. Without anesthesia."

"You and me both, sobrina. You and me both." Dávila put on his hat. "Stay here, you two." He started walking away, then turned back and added with his index finger waggling, "Especially you!"

Javier swallowed. "Me, sir?"

Dávila scoffed. "No, not you, Utierre. Her!" He pointed at his niece. "She's the troublemaker." Then he smiled and walked toward the clamoring press.

Chapter Five

Lupe

GREAT. NOW HER uncle had gone and left her alone with Javier. Lupe never was very good at uncomfortable situations. Or forgiveness. But if she thought about it, what had Javier really done? He had been super cranky since their reunion. Well, not at first. That was nice. But the island, his home, had just been put through the wringer. Besides, it wasn't like she'd never been cranky before—for her that was just Tuesday. But she hadn't liked the jealousy piece. To her that meant a lack of trust, and that she couldn't abide.

Javier coughed. "I have to get back to work."

"Okay. I'll walk you back to the truck." Now that he was leaving, she didn't want him to go. This was *way* too complicated. Her life was so much easier before romance.

The area was now crowded with onlookers, police, some local boy who had been the last to see the victims, cars. They walked along the shore to avoid the press of people, but it was too narrow for them to walk side by side, so she followed behind, looking at the back of his head and trying to think of something to say. They picked their way through the brush and the finger-like reach of the mangrove roots. Soon they were walking along a ridge several feet above the water, and Lupe was concentrating on not tripping when she noticed something hanging off a low branch. She stopped and squatted down.

"What is it? Are you okay, Lupe?"

"Yeah, there's just . . . something here." She looked closely and saw it was fabric of some kind. "It looks like rubberized fabric."

Javier squatted down next to her, his bronzed leg brushing hers, and the warmth made it hard to concentrate.

"It's a piece of a wet suit."

"A wet suit?"

Javier shrugged. "Yeah, people dive around the island all the time."

"Wait, the water is, like, body temperature. Why would they need a suit?"

"I don't know. Guess it depends on how deep they're going."

Lupe looked over the edge of the ridge and saw indentations in the hardened mud. "I see something else. Give me a hand." She moved to the edge, took Javier's hand, and lowered herself into what turned out to be a cove-like area that was hidden by the maze of roots above.

She crouched down and looked at distinct footprints in the dirt. Men's, by the look of them.

Javier's face appeared at the edge of the hidden gap in the shoreline. "What do you see?"

"There are footprints here."

"Human?"

"Yes." She turned around slowly; the prints disappeared where the tide had come in overnight. "Boots, from the look of them. And the prints can't be that old."

"I think we better tell your uncle about this." Javier reached down to help pull her up to the higher shore. She took his hand and let him, something she didn't used to be good at, but *she* trusted *him*.

When she got to higher ground, she stumbled a bit trying to right herself, and Javier steadied her by holding her upper arms, and for a moment they were close. Really close. It would be so easy to just lean in, to feel his arms around her, to press her lips to his again. But instead she stepped back, a small gesture, but she could tell from his reaction that he caught the meaning.

Javier stayed there, standing along the shore, staring into the dark water as if something were crouching there, as she fetched her uncle.

She led Esteban back, showed him the wet suit scrap.

"Could be from anyone, but we'll test it just in case." He put on gloves and stowed the fabric in a plastic bag, handing it off to a CSI who had come with him. Then all three of them scrambled down to the hidden cove to look at the prints. Her uncle pushed his hat back from his forehead.

He was just standing there, not saying anything. She felt like she was going to burst. Finally, she asked, "Do you think this could be from a human bad guy?"

"Definitely a possibility. I had the feeling that this was not the work of ghosts or monsters or zombies."

She crossed her arms. "That's what you said the last time."

"Yes, but it's not like I don't believe in ghosts. My abuela used to sit on the edge of my bed every night after she died. I could feel her weight, see the indentation of where she had sat after."

"You're kidding me."

"Oh, I don't kid about ghosts. But I think these boys were killed by a human or humans. And since I'm pretty sure ghosts don't need boots—"

"Or leave prints," she added.

"I'm thinking these prints might help prove that."

"Dávila!" A loud voice bellowed from above.

"¡Ya voy! I'm coming," her uncle yelled back. He grabbed a vine from the overhanging mangrove tree and pulled himself up with ease. How did he do that? Wasn't he supposed to be old? Before he could help her up, she did the same, feeling a bit like Tarzan as she swung herself up next to him, followed soon after by Javier.

A short, stout man whose flesh seemed barely contained in what was on others a crisp black uniform was stalking over to them. Given the gold trim on his shoulders, Lupe assumed he was the local in charge.

"Dávila, what's going on here? Where are you taking our bodies?"

Her uncle gave him that withering look that she so enjoyed seeing him give *other* people. "First of all, you will address me as Chief Dávila"—his eyes darted to the marks of rank on the man's shoulders as if in judgment—"Captain . . ." He waited for the name.

Just then a younger officer—where did he come from?—reached around the man and saluted her uncle. He was thinner, and his skin a lighter tone than the older man, but they had the same intense, deep-set eyes. Related, had to be. "Torres, Chief. This is Captain Torres, and"—he turned to Lupe and Javier, including them in the introductions—"I'm Hernán Torres . . . his son. I mean, Officer Torres. At your service."

Lupe had to smile. Hernán was clearly not much older than Javier and, unlike his grumpy father, seemed to have a lot of enthusiasm. He was also kind of cute, in an overly clean-cut sort of way.

"Well, Captain Torres, they are not 'your' bodies; they are being taken to the mainland to be autopsied."

"Oh, so you think the local police can't handle this, huh? You had to come and save us all from our ineptitude?"

"Actually, Torres . . ." Lupe noticed the omission of rank. Yeah, he was getting pissed. "*Your* office called *me*."

"What? We most certainly did not!"

"Actually Papá, I called him." The younger Torres's voice was smaller than it was in his introductions, with a touch of nerves on the edges.

His father wheeled around. "What?"

Hernán shrugged. "What with the big opening event coming up and all the townspeople talking about zombies—"

Lupe loved all these mentions of zombies. She had been beginning to think they were extinct and classified as cliché. Hernán was talking quickly, trying to get it out before his father stormed off, a good bet, given the man's demeanor.

"—so I thought we should bring in an expert in the supernatural . . ."

"Expert, hah!" Both Captain Torres and her uncle scoffed at the same time.

Torres Senior pointed his finger at Esteban. He actually had to point up, as he was a good foot shorter. The man just didn't seem to get it. "You look here, Chief . . ." The word dripped with sarcasm as slow as maple syrup. "We have a big event coming up, the biggest in Puerto Rico since the four-hundred-year anniversary in 1992, and we can't have your people traipsing around causing unnecessary complications!"

"Oh, is that what you call this investigation of three dead boys? An 'unnecessary complication'?"

"If you ask me, it's payback for their fathers' destruction of this island! Why they're ripping—"

"Dad . . ." Hernán stepped between the two men. Bold move: she kinda liked this guy. Lupe thought he probably had to play diplomat for his father often. She didn't have to do it much since her father stopped drinking, but she'd played that role enough in her day to understand it well. But why wouldn't the captain want help solving this crime? Investors' children having their hearts torn out couldn't be very good for the tourist trade.

But her uncle only looked amused as the young officer held one hand in front of him and one in front of his stout father, as if Esteban couldn't just crush them both with one move. What an incredible waste of energy.

Javier touched her shoulder. "Lupe," he whispered as the grown men bickered in front of them, "I have to get back to work or I'm going to get my ass fired."

She nodded and turned around. "Just your ass?"

He screwed up his face, "Huh?"

"Not the rest of you?"

He shrugged. "Hard to work with no culo, right?"

She smiled. "Maybe." She was trying to lighten it up between them, she knew she was. He probably knew it too, but Lupe just didn't know how to work around Javier's anger. She'd always been attracted to angry boys, surely because the men in her family were angry men, but it was also because she liked the passion, the willingness to fight to change things that weren't right. She'd never tolerate angry, *violent* men, but she liked boys who felt things deeply. But this? The anger coming off Javier in waves like radiation was hard to navigate.

They reached his truck and she realized they'd walked all that way without saying a word. Damn.

Javier stopped and scuffed the sand with his shoe. "When do you go back to your uncle's in Guaynabo?"

"Not for a few days. Tío rented a condo so we could stay here while he works on the case."

He nodded, hesitated, then said, "I'm glad you're back, Lupe." But he wasn't looking at her. Why wouldn't he look at her?

"Me, too." She flipped thoughts over and over in her mind like discarded cards. What was the right thing to say? How could she help him?

"Okay." He paused, then opened his driver's side door and slipped in, pulling the dented door closed behind him.

"Okay." Her heart was pounding, the blood and water and life being squeezed out of it. Was she losing him? Why? He wasn't looking at her, so she turned around and started back toward her uncle, tears brimming against her eyelids.

She heard the engine roar to life, and the truck start to rattle away. Then it stopped with a spray of sand. "Lupe!" A yell this time.

She turned around and saw him looking at her. "Would you like to come on a dinner picnic with me on the beach tonight?"

Lupe took a deep, catchy breath. How could her heart stand such wild swings from one side to the other? And a nighttime beach picnic? Sounded like something out of a teen romance novel. She wouldn't miss it for the world. "Sure" was all she said, and as she turned to keep walking, a smile came unbidden, the tears forgotten.

All was not lost.

Chapter Six

Javier

JAVIER CHECKED BEHIND the seat for what seemed like the hundredth time: picnic basket of food, blanket, cooler of soda. He hadn't forgotten anything. This had to be just right. Perfect, even. He needed a night with Lupe that brought them as close as they'd felt before. He'd almost chickened out of asking her, but when he found out she would be staying for a few days he figured it was worth a shot; she was worth more than his ego. He was thrilled when she'd said yes, but now he wondered if it was a mistake. He hadn't been particularly good company lately. Staying on the island, banging on stone, and working in the sun had been an excuse to not deal with people at all. It didn't help that he was working for the very people who were buying up land in the island's darkest hour. However, he'd grown attached to eating and being able to gas up his car. When there *was* gas, that is. The lines at the stations after the hurricane had only started moving a few months ago. He'd never take fuel for granted again.

He pulled up in front of the whitewashed condos, freshly repainted after the battering of Maria. He had barely rolled to a stop when Lupe came bounding out the front door in a short white dress, the fabric billowing behind, her strong legs ending in slip-on sneakers.

She was so damn cute.

She pulled herself up into the truck's passenger seat, and Javier inhaled her scent of soap and Vermont woods.

"Hi." A small smile from her. He'd take it.

"Hi. Ready?" He put the car in Drive and did a U-turn, but when the truck finished the turn, an old man appeared in the road right in front of them. Javier slammed on the brakes, his heart pounding in his chest.

"Jesus! Where did he come from?" Lupe asked in a breathy voice.

The old man glared at them with his cloudy eyes, shaking a fist. His clothes weren't more than rags, his hair falling in long white wisps like corn silk. In his unfisted hand he clutched a dark bottle. Only when he was safely on the sidewalk did Javier start moving again. A litany of obscenities in English and Spanish followed them down the street.

"Well, he was pleasant," Lupe quipped.

Javier's heart was racing from the almost accident, but he took a deep breath and it slowed. "Hard to know what he's been through. So many people lost so much."

A beat of silence, then, "Where are we going?"

He'd expected this question. She wasn't the blind follower type. But he wasn't going to give in.

"It's a surprise. A place I found last week."

They made their way on the secondary roads. Well, actually, there weren't really any primary roads. Vieques was several decades behind the mainland and the residents liked it that way. They were on narrow dirt roads, passing by small dilapidated shacks with sparse, deep pink bougainvillea blooms weaving in the front gates. The poor had been hit so much harder during the storm, most of the buildings were covered in the familiar blue FEMA tarps where the roofs used to be. After all of this was over, and if the island ever did fully recover, he hoped to never see that particular color blue ever again.

Then even those houses thinned and there was nothing but green on either side. The top of the brush had gotten sheared off during the hurricane, but the greens were coming back with a vengeance.

They weren't talking, but that was okay. Last summer they had gotten into the habit of driving around the main island, windows down, music playing, Lupe sniffing the air out the window like a puppy, eyes closed, a huge smile on her face. He loved seeing the island through her eyes. She was in love with it all: the smell of the salty air, the colors, the song of the coquís. It became new when he was with her. But she couldn't understand how close they'd come to losing it all just a few short months ago, and he found his thoughts turning that way more often than not when he talked with her.

The road got bumpier as they neared their destination, cups and papers flying around the cab. *Why didn't I clean the inside of the truck?* he thought. It felt like a first date. They pushed through a clearing in the trees and the hidden beach stretched out before them, a cove of vanilla-colored sand surrounded by nearly undamaged trees with pale turquoise water lapping the shores. He'd timed it perfectly; the sky was turning a rich orange. Lupe gasped beside him, and he smiled at the desired response.

"I . . . I've never seen a beach this . . . perfect! I mean, other than in a calendar, or something." Her blue eyes were large, her body leaned toward the windshield as if pulled by the waves.

"I hadn't either. I just found it one night when I was driving around after work. I haven't told anyone about it. Other than you."

"Let's go check it out!" Her voice had that childlike glee he so loved. Then she was opening the door and slipping onto the sand, ripping her sneakers off as she ran.

He grabbed the basket of food, blanket, and cooler, and climbed out to follow. Lupe was galloping toward the water's edge, leaving sprays of sand behind her. He laid out the blanket, securing the corners with the basket and cooler, and went to join her.

"This is unbelievable!" she yelled into the wind. She looked at Javier. "I don't understand, why aren't there tons of obnoxious tourists here? This is even more amazing than beaches on the mainland. And they're amazing!"

He shrugged. "I guess because it's harder to get to the island, and especially hard to find this location. I didn't see it on any of the maps. This whole part of the island was occupied by the U.S. Navy for years, and now it's a nature preserve."

"Well, I'm glad you found it." She looked back at him, her eyes sparkling in the setting sun. "Thank you for taking me here."

He smiled, feeling the heat rise behind his face, and other places. But he wasn't going to rush anything. He changed the subject. "Are you hungry?" he asked, and pointed toward the basket on the blanket.

She clapped her hands. "Yes! I love picnics! Food always tastes better outdoors." And then she was bounding back, dropping herself on the blanket, and peeking in the basket. He couldn't stop smiling. She really was like a little kid sometimes, and he loved that about her.

They chatted back and forth as they ate, talking about Vieques, catching up on news of Carlos and Marisol, the friends they had in common, their families.

"How are things going with your father? I mean, not drinking and all?"

She didn't answer right away, which was unlike her. In conversation it often felt like she was bursting with all the things she wanted to say, all the ideas she had. He wondered if he shouldn't have asked, if her father had fallen off the wagon and that's why she hadn't been talking about herself much in the last few months. But then she gave him a small smile as she folded and refolded a napkin.

"It's good." Folding, refolding. "You know, I wished for him to stop drinking most of my life." Folding, refolding. Then she looked up at Javier. "Don't get me wrong, it's great. I'm so happy he's sober, but it didn't solve all our problems, you know? We still fight. A lot." She picked up the napkin and tore it. "All of a sudden he wants to parent me? Like, get involved in my life after being drunk and not present for most of it? Yeah, no thanks."

He watched her for a moment more, leaving room for her to say more if she wanted to. When she didn't, he spoke. "Yeah, I'm sure he wished he could undo it all. I did. But you can't turn back the clock." His words sounded hollow to his ears, but she seemed to hear them.

They sat quietly for a few minutes, the lap of the waves and the light wind in the trees overhead the only sounds as the sun was glowing a deeper orange, then red beyond the horizon. It was pretty much perfect. Javier chose another half a sandwich and took a bite with a sigh.

Lupe looked around the cove, up and down the beach, at the trees behind them. "It's interesting, from this spot you almost can't tell the hurricane happened."

He stopped chewing and looked at her.

"I mean, the trees aren't that damaged—the cove must have protected them. You could almost forget."

Javier felt heat build behind his face. He thought about the damage inside his chest that no one could see. The hours and hours huddling in the bathroom with his mother while the house roared around them. It had seemed like it would never stop, that they had stepped into some endless loop of a nightmare. The fear he had experienced when he'd walked around his hometown, Amapola, and seen houses destroyed, children with signs begging for water. "Almost," he said under his breath, pulling back into himself. Sometimes she seemed to understand everything, and then other times . . .

Lupe didn't miss his response. She put her hand on his. "I didn't mean any disrespect. I can imagine—"

"No, you can't!" He was shocked by the volume and fury of his voice. "No one in the States can understand what it was like. I mean, the president comes down for a few hours, throws paper towels, then downplays the amount of dead?"

She pulled back as if from a blow. Her voice was measured. "I wasn't happy with his response either. My family was also impacted—"

"Yes, I know, but your family and mine? We had the resources to have generators, and gas; most people didn't. When you can't even get water to drink—" He sputtered, the words gathering up behind one another at the tip of his tongue.

She waited for a moment, just looking at the uneaten sandwich in her hand. Then she said in a quiet but steady voice, "Look, Javier, I'm sorry. I didn't mean to sound insensitive. But my uncle was out on the streets the entire time with the police and rescue force, my father and I sat by the phone, watching the news—"

"Yes, from the safety of your house in Vermont with power to run the refrigerator and water coming out of the tap, and ATMs and cell service. No rats coming up from the flooded sewers, running across your mother's floors . . ." His breath ran out and he put his head in his hands.

He could tell she was staring at him; he could feel it. Then she was putting the leftover food back in the basket with sharp, quick movements.

No; this was going all wrong. "Lupe, I'm sorry, I—"

But she kept going. "Maybe this was a mistake. I shouldn't have come." Tears were glistening on her eyelashes and Javier wondered how he could feel any worse. Not sure what to do, he started to close up the cooler, his heart beating on the inside of his rib cage like it was telling him to stop.

They had both stood and begun to gather the edges of the blanket when Lupe stopped short and stared toward the trees in the growing darkness.

He followed her gaze. "What? Do you see something?" he whispered.

"Javier, do you see that?" She pointed into the trees next to the road they had driven in on.

When he saw what she was pointing at, he knew the night had truly gone to hell.

Chapter Seven

Lupe

THE BLUE GLOW was coming from deep within the trees, and Lupe couldn't take her eyes off it. "Do you . . . do you think it's them? What everyone has been seeing?" she whispered.

"I don't know what else it could be."

But the light was dimming, getting more distant.

Javier let out a breath next to her. "Thank God, they're moving away from us."

But she started walking toward the light. Finally, a way she could help.

"Lupe, what are you doing?"

"I want to see them. Let's get closer. C'mon!"

Javier stood firm. "You're serious."

"Of course!" She could see he wasn't buying it, and for a moment, one moment, she wondered if he was right. He was the stable one, after all. "Look, Javier, where would the El Cuco investigation have been without us, huh? Don't you want to see what this is about?"

He shrugged a bit, and she knew she had appealed to his curiosity. "Yeah, but what if they are the ones taking hearts? I'm quite attached to mine," he said, hand to his chest.

"They won't even know we're there; I just want to get a look to see what we're dealing with. C'mon, Detective." He smiled back and she knew she had him. She held out her hand for him to take. This was her kind of date.

He clasped her hand and they made their way to the tree line, slowly and silently. She could see the haze of the blue glow in the distance like a beacon. Step by step, they picked their way into the trees, careful not to trip on any roots or branches. The dried leaves beneath their feet made small, crisp sounds, but the wind and the crashing waves provided cover.

When they were several yards away, the sun fully set and dark covered all but whatever or whoever was glowing, so they stopped behind a palm trunk and watched.

Javier whispered into her ear and a tingling sensation spread throughout her body. Damn, was she, like, turned on by danger?

"They're definitely people, or the shapes of them."

At first it seemed to be one mass, a band of light, but then it broke into dozens of individual figures, glowing slightly blue like the bio-bay waters, as Lupe saw what Javier saw. It was a swarm of people, ghostly and glowing, moving among the trees. Lupe and Javier couldn't see their faces since they were walking away, but the women wore longish skirts that brushed the ground in tatters. The men were dressed in suits, or the remnants of them, some with the remains of hats on their heads. Their hair was not unlike the old man they'd almost run over, long and wispy. There was even a little girl in a once-frilly dress, with rotten bows in her hair, holding the skeletal hand of the woman next to her, an eyeless doll dangling from her other hand.

"They don't look like zombies. I'm thinking ghosts, don't you agree?" She turned around to look at Javier, the blue of the supernatural beings sparkling in his eyes.

He nodded. "Definitely fantasmas."

The glow was moving away en masse into the trees in the distance. "Are we going to follow them?" Javier asked.

Lupe looked around. They had no flashlights, no water, and Lord knew if the swarm was dangerous or not. "Nah, I'm curious, not stupid. Let's go back and tell my uncle."

They had just started to turn around when Carlos's hit song blared from Javier's pocket, the thrumming beat echoing off the trees.

He yanked it from his pocket and silenced it. He looked at Lupe and whispered, "*Now* I get service?"

It was the rustling sound that reached them first. Their heads shot back in the direction of the glow to see the entire group stop and slowly turn back to face them.

For one second, Javier and Lupe and the ghostly swarm just stared at one another.

Then, they started coming.

"Oh shit."

Javier yelled, "Run!"

And they did. Lupe could feel the sand shifting under her bare feet as they pounded. They had gone farther than she realized, but finally she could see the silhouette of the pickup truck, waiting in the distance.

Then, on the early evening breeze, she heard the sound of moaning.

She made the mistake of looking back, she could see Javier did too, and there the swarm was, going slower, but still getting closer. They weren't running, more like skimming over the surface of the earth. That was just not fair!

"Get to the truck!" Javier yelled, as if that were ever in question.

Lupe's legs were burning, her breaths coming short and fast, fear flaming through her lungs. Javier made it to the truck first, yanking open the doors. Lupe was a few yards away when she felt something on the back of her neck, like a spiderweb. She brushed at it and spun around to find a woman, or what was left of one, right behind her. Her eye sockets were empty and black, but Lupe knew she was looking at her, moans coming from her hinged jaws in waves. But it was her fingers that Lupe was focused on, her long, thin, bony fingers that had dusty strips of flesh on them, skeletal white peeking through in the starlight. Those fingers, hands, were reaching for Lupe, reaching for her chest, bones clicking, probing.

Was she reaching for Lupe's heart? Then she was just . . . gone, but Lupe could see her back with the masses who were coming closer.

"Lupe, c'mon!" Javier bellowed from the truck, the sound of the ignition trying to fire accompanying him.

She lurched back, almost tripping on the sand dune below the truck, then caught her balance, tore up the dune, and leapt into the passenger seat of the truck.

"Go! Go!" she yelled at him, as if he needed to hear that.

Javier pumped the gas and turned the key again. A grinding noise, like metal teeth.

No. Not happening, Lupe thought.

Javier said a quick prayer under his breath and turned the key again.

It didn't turn over.

Lupe stared out the window. They were going to be trapped. She breathed, "Javier, I think we better run."

"No, no, it will start."

Turn, grind, stop.

Turn, grind, stop.

He was flooding it now, and they both knew it. Hell, the ghosts probably knew it. Javier bashed on the steering wheel with his fists. "Damn you, Pedro! What a piece of shit!"

Lupe pulled on his sleeve and pointed out the back window. The figures were only a few feet away, and she could see their faces, cheekbones jutting out, covered with desiccated flesh, empty eye sockets. They were all reaching now, their sharp, bony fingers leading the way

"It's not going to start. Let's get out of here." And they were out of the truck, both tearing across the moonlit beach, trying to focus on what was ahead and not on the ghostly figures behind them.

They were halfway across when Javier stopped short. "Wait, I don't know which way we should go. What if we're at the tip of the island?"

Lupe stopped, but almost tripped on a weather- and salt-eaten board on the beach. "What is this?" She picked it up and her breath stopped. It was a sign, and after reading it she put her free hand out in front of Javier. "Don't take another step," she whispered.

"What? Why?" He was looking back at the glowing figures with increasing anxiety. She turned the sign around to show him.

He read it out loud. CAUTION: UNEXPLODED ORDNANCE. KEEP OUT!

She knew unexploded was bad. "What the hell is an ordnance?"

"I am guessing this was one of the beaches the navy used to test weapons. Lupe, ordnance is bombs or grenades or land mines—"

"Okay, okay," she whispered, as if merely the vibration of her voice could set them off. "I get it." She glanced from the stretch of beach between them and the trees, and back at the . . . beings coming for them, their moans riding the sounds of the surf and reaching for them. "What do we do now?"

They looked back. Only a few yards remained between them and the beings. Thank god they moved slowly. "I'm not the expert on the supernatural that you are, but I'm imagining they don't have to worry about the bombs, right?"

Lupe shrugged. "That would be my guess."

"Well, shit."

They both looked toward the water. The tide had come in and the waves were increasing in intensity. Plus, the cove was edged in rock cliffs. No way they could swim for it.

Something brushed against Lupe's neck again, and she yelped. She turned around slowly to find a large, shadowy face nuzzling the side of her head. It took a second before she realized it was the long furry snout of a dark brown horse.

She ran her hand along his nose. "Hi, sweetie," she cooed. The horse was shaking his head toward the ghosts who were only feet away now. "Javier, how did he make it through?"

"I don't know." Then he seemed to remember something. "On this nature show I watch, in Cambodia they use rats to sniff out the land mines. Maybe he can sense them too."

"Or maybe he's just been lucky," Lupe said while petting the scruffy creature's head. "Does he belong to someone nearby, maybe? Someone who can help?"

"No, I don't think so. There are wild horses all over the island."

The moaning picked up in intensity and the ghosts were close to Javier now, fingers reaching toward his chest. He and Lupe were both frozen in place, afraid to run and set off a mine, but unable to stay.

The horse sniffed, then started to turn around, looking back toward Lupe, then shaking his head up and down like he was nodding, his mane waving in the moonlight. She watched him carefully. "I think he's trying to tell us something. I think he wants to lead us out," she whispered.

Javier threw up his hands. "Well, let's follow him. We don't have any other choice."

Lupe followed behind the horse at an appropriate distance—she'd done enough riding in Vermont that she knew you didn't want to be within kicking range if the horse got spooked—and took Javier's hand behind her. They walked single file, stepping carefully into the horse's tracks, the moaning and rustling a constant companion behind them to remind them of the urgency. With each step Lupe imagined a blast of fire, her legs flying around the empty beach, setting off other mines as they landed, the sand exploding in a cloud of smoke and flame.

Her dramatic imagination was a bit of a drag at times.

She looked up and realized they were already to the tree line and the horse had begun to run. Without a word, they followed behind, rushing through breaks in the trees and the trampled brush that the horse left behind, branches flying back and scratching along her cheeks and arms as they gained distance between themselves and the ghost-infested beach. They staggered into a clearing, and the horse slowed, then stopped, then began chewing on some long grass in front of a ramshackle house. There was the light of a single lamp inside, and as the moon rose above the trees, Lupe could make out a figure on the porch, the glow of a cigar tip red in the darkness.

This was just like something in a horror movie, but Javier stepped forward. Lupe looked around the clearing, the hurricane-stripped palm branches like thin fingers reaching up to the sky, the moonlight giving the ring of trees a blue glow like the ghosts. No way was she going to stand there by herself, so she followed Javier.

A crackly voice rose from the porch's shadow. "You children look like you've seen a ghost! Or perhaps many ghosts!" Then came a cackle, loud and bordering on out of control, the sound bouncing off the surrounding trees.

Lupe wondered if they had just jumped from the frying pan into the fire.

Chapter Eight

Javier

AT THE SOUND of the creepy cackling, Javier grabbed Lupe's hand and took an involuntary step back before he remembered the crowd of undead who had been following them, and then stepped toward the unknown character on the porch. At least the old man seemed to be alive. The bomb-sensing horse seemed calm, so he took that as a sign they could relax.

A little.

The laughing slowed, then stopped, followed by the sound of a deep drag of breath and the flaring of the cigar's tip. Then the unseen man was hacking, like his lungs were coming out his mouth. Finally, he said, "Well? Who are you and what are you doing on my property?"

"Perdón, señor."

"Chachu."

"Salud," Lupe responded. "Bless you."

The old man just growled at her. "No, that's what they call me, young lady. Chachu."

Lupe's face reddened.

Javier continued, "Chachu, we were on that beach." He

pointed back toward the beach with the unexploded ordnance. "We didn't know it was dangerous. Then these . . . well, they were . . ." He was trying to find a respectful way to say it when Lupe broke in.

"A herd of ghosts chased us off the beach. And your horse there saved us by leading us here."

Javier waited for the cackling to resume. It sounded so damn bizarre even to him, and he'd just lived through it.

Instead, another long drag on the cigar, then a sigh. "She's not my horse, she doesn't belong to anyone."

"That's what he chose to respond to?" Lupe whispered. She wasn't helping. Then louder. "So . . . the fact that I just told you we were chased by a bunch of ghosts is no surprise?"

"Young lady, I've lived on this island for every one of my eighty-seven years, and nothing surprises me anymore."

Javier took a step closer. "Did you hear about the murders in Mosquito Bay?"

Chachu nodded. Javier could tell by the glowing tip going up and down. Then Chachu leaned forward and his wrinkled face caught the moonlight, his eye sockets darkening as if empty like the ghosts'.

Javier didn't trust him yet.

Chachu took another drag of his cigar, the sweet, cherry-smelling smoke wafting from under the porch roof. "I know who those ghosts are."

Lupe muttered, "Oh. Great. He knows the ghosts personally. This is only getting creepier and creepier."

But Javier was captivated. He knew the value of people like this, the viejos who sat on their porches as life went by. They often knew everything that was happening on the island, didn't miss a thing. He walked toward the porch and, after hesitating, Lupe followed him.

Javier's eyes were adjusting to the darkness, and as they

stopped and stood in front of the man he saw how thin he was, how withered. Javier prodded him. "So, who are they, Señor?"

"Oh, I think they're people who have been here all along."

Javier worked at keeping his patience—the man was, like, one hundred and fourteen years old—but it was tough. It had been a very long night.

Lupe snorted. "Okay, moving on."

She was right: they were wasting their time there. He thought back to the scene on the beach: they had to get out of here soon in case the ghosts were following. He took the cell phone out of his pocket and turned it on, this time with the ringer off.

No service.

Perfecto.

"Señor, do you have a phone we could use?"

He waved his hand. "Bah! What do I need one of those for? Only people who call me are trying to sell me something! Or buy my land!"

Javier sighed; it was going to be a long walk. "How far is it to town?"

"Oh, it's a long walk, with many hills. Why don't you leave your girlfriend here to keep an old man company while you walk to town?"

He waggled his thick, unruly white eyebrows. Actually waggled them.

"I just threw up in my mouth a bit," Lupe whispered. "There is no way I'm staying here with that creep."

Javier shook his head, a small smile lifting the corner of his mouth. "No, we're going to stay together."

He put his arm around her protectively, and she wrapped her arm around his waist, tight. "I guess we better get walking, Lupe."

The old man took another drag. "You could do that. Take you quite a while in the dark."

Not to mention the undead horde that could be waiting for them.

This *was* going to be a long night.

"Or, I could give you a lift in Estrellita." Then there were two electronic beeps and headlights beamed toward them and they noticed the late-model Kia in fire-engine red that sat placidly next to Chachu's ramshackle house.

This night was just full of surprises.

Chapter Nine

Isabel Segunda, Vieques

MORTIMER CARTER WAS angry. Not about anything in particular, though he'd almost been run over by some young hooli-
gans that afternoon. No, it was pretty much his default state.
There was so much to be angry about these days. Since he'd
retired and moved full time to his late aunt's house on this
godforsaken island, everything pissed him off. And that had
been, oh, twenty-five years back, now.

He stumbled through the darkened streets, heading home
after a failed attempt to buy another bottle of moonshine. The
bastard who made it had closed up for the night, the house
all dark. It wasn't even past midnight yet, and he was closed?
Mortimer had pounded on the door for a good ten minutes
until the shrew next door yelled out the window, her spoiled
baby shrieking in the background. Well, he told her a thing or
two and kept pounding for another ten minutes, just because
she pissed him off.

Nothing went smoothly on this damn island. Everyone
moved slowly, no work ethic in these people, no hustle. But
damned if he was going to stay in North Carolina while his

lazy-ass grandnephew tried to get his paws on his money. No sirree Bob! He was keeping it all in an offshore account where it was safe, and after the land sale he just made, he had a lot to protect.

He felt the brush of something across the back of his neck. "Who the hell is there?" he shrieked, wheeling around. Did he see something duck between the buildings? No, probably a rat, or something. Probably all this talk about ghosts was causing hallucinations. Whole damn island was going crazy. *Ghosts, sheesh! Next thing you know, Godzilla will be crawling up on Esperanza Beach!*

Mortimer stumbled on the broken sidewalk, cursing loudly. *Goddamn town doesn't even take care of its streets. They're using the hurricane as an excuse.* Well, he'd lived through a few of those; in fact his aunt bought the cursed house and all that land after the hurricane of '28. And they didn't whine about damage in those days. They just fixed it! Well, in the morning he would give that pudgy Torres police captain a piece of his mind. Maybe he'd take a piece of the concrete and pitch it through the bastard's car window! Would serve him right.

He paused by the house next door to catch his breath. Damn humidity was causing his asthma to act up. He glanced at the neighbor's house and half expected that bitch to be on the porch, nattering at him as he went by. Always going on and on about the condition of his house. If she'd use her big mouth to bitch about the sidewalks maybe they wouldn't be in such terrible condition!

He went to take a step, but the wind picked up and swirled around him, howling. Or was it a moan? He shivered. Should have had his sweater, damn it! But that laundry woman was late with getting him his clothes back. Hurricane shoulda carried them all off and left him alone.

A sound across the street. A stone, or something like it.

There *was* somebody following, he knew it! Probably a mugger trying to steal his money, and right across the street from his own house! Well, he wasn't afraid. He hobbled as fast as his aching legs could carry him. He had been a Golden Gloves boxing champion in his day; he could fight twice as hard as someone half his age. He'd show them.

He stopped on the sidewalk and peered toward where he'd heard the noise. His eyes weren't too good in the dark anymore. The sound . . . it came from by that abandoned house, the one with the fencing around it.

"I know you're there! Come out and fight like a man!" He held his fists up in a classic boxing stance. He hadn't lost it!

Movement on the other side of the building. Mortimer shuffled quickly, determined to catch whoever it was in the act. As he walked, he noticed a broken bottle on the ground near the fence. He picked it up and held it in his quaking hand. He wasn't going down without a fight, that was for damn sure.

Then a shadow on the side started moving toward him, slow but steady, otherworldly like. When he realized what it was, his knees gave way and he fell to the sidewalk.

"Y-you? But that's impossible, I—"

The last thing he felt was his head bumping over rocks and broken glass as he was dragged over the cracks in the sidewalk.

Then darkness fell.

Chapter Ten

Lupe

☠

THERE IT WAS again. Lupe sat up and listened. She thought the knocking was part of her dream, but no such luck. She grabbed her cell phone to check the time.

Two a.m.

She was willing to bet big money that whoever it was, they weren't looking for her. And she knew from spending last summer with her uncle that door knocking at this hour was never good.

She flipped off the sheets and tiptoed into the living room. Her uncle wasn't in his room. He had fallen asleep sitting up, still in his clothes, the television glowing with some random cop show. He'd told her he loved to watch fictional crime dramas because they weren't his problem. "Let them wake up someone else for a change," he would say, laughing. Well, clearly that change wasn't tonight. She stood over her uncle, enjoying the rare moment of looking down on the tall man, and shook him gently as he snored.

"Tío."

Shake.

"Tío."

Shake harder.

A knock again. She sighed in frustration.

"Tío!" she yelled, right in his face.

He jolted up in the chair, the remote flying across the room. "¡Madre de Dios! What? What's wrong?" He looked around, obviously confused.

She couldn't stifle a giggle. It was so rare to catch him off guard; this was *so* entertaining. "Someone's knocking, and given the hour, I don't think it's a pizza delivery."

He wiped his big hand down his face as if swiping away the sleep, stood up, and gave her a chastising look. "Was the yelling necessary? You scared me half to death."

"Almost as badly as you scared me when I came in tonight and you were standing next to the front door."

"Yes, well, I said you could go out with Javier; I didn't think you'd get back in the middle of the night." Another knock. "¡Voy!" he yelled, slipping on his shoes.

"It was barely midnight . . . ish."

He looked back at her with narrowed eyes as he started toward the door, but then he stopped, turned around, and grabbed his gun belt from the coffee table, buckling it around his waist as he walked.

She gave him the side-eye. "Really? You think that's necessary for answering the door?"

"These days you never know, sobrina."

"Point taken."

He yanked open the door and the young woman standing there jumped back, her eyes going huge.

"Lo siento, Chief, I'm sorry to disturb you." Her voice was quiet and shaky. Clearly knocking on the door at that hour was not her idea.

Her uncle used his extra-patient voice. "It's fine, joven. What's wrong?"

"My mother asked me to come get you. She found one of our neighbors, the old gringo . . . well, she found him in the garden. It's his heart."

An old man has a heart attack and they wake them up? To his credit, her uncle stayed calm and patient. "Found him? Did you call an ambulance?"

Lupe hoped this would mean just a call and they could go back to bed. Her head was foggy with sleep.

"No, Señor. An ambulance cannot help him now. His heart . . . it's gone."

Lupe gasped and the girl noticed her and nodded.

Okay, that bit of information woke them up. She could see her uncle go into full cop mode. He grabbed his hat and started out the door, Lupe on his tail.

He looked back at her as she closed the door behind them. "And where do you think you're going?"

Lupe looked down at her pajamas. A T-shirt and shorts. Perfectly acceptable. "You would think by now you'd know, Tío. There's no scenario where I don't end up going with you, so you might as well accept it."

He let out a deep sigh. "True." He looked over at the door-knocking girl. "Lead the way, joven."

They walked in a line and Lupe rubbed her arms, surprised at the cool evening air. It was cooler on the small island, the winds coming off the waters of both the Atlantic and the Ca-ribbean Sea. The streets were deserted, made up of variations of the color of slate with sharp edges in the dark, like a film-noir movie set. Lupe took a deep breath, feeling her heart slow from the rush of the middle-of-the-night door knock. Her uncle once told her that he didn't mind being woken up in the middle of the night. Looking around, she understood why. This time of the morning was crisp and silent, the op-posite of the summer days in Puerto Rico. This part of town had streetlights, but more than half were blown out, some crowned by shards of broken glass, probably from Maria, the broken bulbs not replaced. Every day she was newly stunned by how much damage the hurricane had caused.

When they turned the corner of a narrow street with crumbling asphalt, there was already a group of locals gathered in a small side yard, a string of laundry dangling over the inert body on the ground, a motion-sensor floodlight flickering on and off. The girl led them over, then peeled off, and the group of onlookers parted for Esteban as if on hinges.

Her uncle crouched beside the body and she stepped closer. Truth was, she'd never seen a dead body in person before. Even with all the death that had surrounded them last summer, the closest she'd gotten was when she had hidden behind the polished wood of a coffin. The old man looked like he was sleeping, except for the fact that his chest cavity was pried open like a picked-clean guinea hen, with an empty space where his heart should have been. There was a surprising lack of blood.

Lupe checked in with herself.

She should have been freaked out, maybe even vomiting. This was not just a dead body, but a mutilated one. But she felt surprisingly calm. In truth, she was fascinated. "Was he killed somewhere else and brought here?"

"It's possible," her uncle answered, then seemed to realize the question had come from her. He looked up at her with a puzzled expression. "How did you know that?"

She shrugged. "Not enough blood around the body."

A small smile teased up one side of his mouth, then he returned his attention to the body.

The man was old, she thought, probably eighty or eighty-five. His skin was pale with a bluish tint, and he had a hunched back and a permanent scowl on his face. Having your heart torn out is reason enough for a scowl, but the lines etched deeply in the man's face gave Lupe the impression that this had been a permanent expression.

Wait.

"I've seen this guy."

Her uncle looked up at her. "Where?"

"Not far from our condo. Javier and I almost hit him with the truck." Wait, that sounded bad. "I mean, not intentionally. He kind of stepped out in front of it." That was better. Slightly. But Esteban didn't seem concerned with that.

Her uncle looked up and around the area. He asked a question of the onlookers: "Did he live near here?"

A small, thin middle-aged lady who looked like an older version of the girl who'd come to get them pointed to the dark house to their left. Esteban stood up, a little carefully as he unbent his tall frame with an audible creak, and walked around the house. Lupe followed him like a shadow. She'd always found her uncle's job fascinating, but watching him work was beyond.

The paint on the small dilapidated house was peeling to the point of nonexistence, and chunks were missing from the cement columns that held up the front porch. He looked over to the right and Lupe followed his gaze. The woman's house next door was neat as a pin, with a tended garden and mismatched but comfortable chairs out front, warm yellow lights glowing from within, and a fresh coat of pink paint.

The damage to the dead man's house was not post-Maria. It showed signs of years of neglect. He had probably been poor and sick, unable to do the necessary work on the house.

She heard clipped footsteps on the stone walk behind them and jumped, just a bit. They both turned to find the local captain's son . . . Hernán, she thought his name was, walking up, his face open in a wide yawn.

"Is the murder disturbing your beauty sleep?" Esteban

asked, but he smiled at the young man. Despite the snide comment, her uncle seemed glad the younger guy was there. She was good company to him, she knew, but she was no cop.

Hernán smiled back sheepishly. "I'm sorry, I just got a call and rushed over." Then he looked over at Lupe and bowed slightly, like she was royalty or something. This guy was a trip. He was growing on her.

"Did you know this man?" Esteban asked as they walked back to the body, watched by the growing crowd of onlookers.

Hernán looked down at the body on the ground and grimaced. "Sí. It's a tiny island, Chief. Everyone knows everyone."

"Even some people we wish we didn't know," a woman said from behind them.

Her uncle whipped around, startling the woman. "And why is that, Señora? Are you referring to the deceased?"

"Yes." She crossed her arms, the fat underneath waggling then settling comfortably against her ample bosom like an old cat. "Señor Carter was an awful little man."

A woman next to her gasped and made the sign of the cross, obviously horrified that she would speak ill of the dead.

"Well I don't care, Imelda! I'm just saying what everyone here always thinks but never says."

Esteban looked around at the crowd, and though they avoided meeting his gaze, it was apparent, even to Lupe, that the woman was telling the truth.

Lupe couldn't stop herself from asking a question. "What was wrong with Mr. Carter?"

"Yes. Why was he an 'awful little man'?"

It was as if a switch had been thrown, and the woman became really animated. As she spoke, Lupe could tell this was a favorite subject of hers.

"He was always complaining about any work we did on our

houses—God forbid someone should actually care for their home—and he was always calling the police when we spent time in our yards, eating, visiting with family. Not wild parties, mind you, and at reasonable hours!"

Another man spoke up, emboldened. "He complained to me about my children playing in the street, that the sound of the basketball hitting the ground and their laughing was too loud. Who complains about children's laughter?" A hum of agreement.

Esteban nodded. "Okay, I get the picture. How long has he lived in this house?"

Someone answered "Twenty, thirty years, at least. He used to only come for the holidays until he retired. His aunt lived there before him. She was unpleasant, too."

The first woman laughed. "And that was the last time he painted the damn house!"

The other woman made the sign of the cross again.

Lupe's uncle turned to her and Hernán and said softly, "But this doesn't fit the pattern of the bio-bay murders. I mean, other than that he's a gringo, too. Those boys were wealthy, entitled outsiders, but this man was old and poor—"

Hernán interjected, speaking low. "Chief, Mr. Carter wasn't poor."

Lupe and Esteban looked back at the decaying house, at the small houses crowded in like sardines along the dirt road.

Lupe spoke up, she couldn't help it. "Wait, what?"

Hernán shook his head. "No, he owned most of this area."

"Since when? Did he just buy it?" Was he taking advantage of people after the hurricane too?

"No, his family bought it in the twenties or thirties. And he has millions in the bank."

Esteban said, "Why on earth would he live so frugally then?"

Hernán shrugged his shoulders. "Cheap, I guess."

The chief looked into the younger man's eyes, and Lupe noticed the few working streetlights lent them a bright glint. Her uncle was giving him that probing look he was so famous for. "How do you know all this?"

"Mr. Carter was always trying to get me to work on his house for free, but a friend who was his accountant told me not to—told me he could more than afford it. When I went back to the States, I took a break from college, apprenticed to an electrician for a while. My mom was constantly on my case to go back to my pre-med studies, but whenever I came home for the holidays, or summers with my father, old man Carter kept insisting I help him. I told him I was studying to be a doctor, not an electrician now, but he was hard to say no to."

There was more to this guy's story, Lupe could tell. After her uncle turned away to speak with the locals, Hernán stayed nearby, so she asked, "What happened? With school, I mean. Why did you become a cop?"

A shadow crossed his face, for just a second. Then it was gone and Lupe wondered if she'd imagined it.

"I lived with my mom, in Chicago, but she and I"—he smirked—"we didn't get along. After Hurricane Maria, a lot of my father's staff left and he needed help. So, Mom sent me to live with him."

Sounded familiar. Her father had started sending her away during the summer so he could drink in peace. "*Didn't* get along? So, you get along now?"

He shook his head. "No, she's dead."

"Oh. I'm sorry." She didn't need to ask anymore, she'd heard enough, but he kept going.

"Now I can't afford to go back to school. I had to commit to five years down here with my father. But I don't think I'll ever leave now." The darkness crossed his face again, but he seemed to recover and smiled and shrugged. "So, here I am: a cop."

Lupe considered him for a second, took in his pale skin, his accentless English. "Your mom, she's not . . . wasn't Puerto Rican, was she?"

A smile, "Nah, I'm half. Half Puerto Rican, half Midwest white bread."

She snorted. "At least you're fluent in Spanish."

"I didn't have much of a choice. My dad insisted. I'm kind of glad, you know?" He looked around them, the sky beginning to lighten at the edges, the crowd thinning as people made their way back to their houses. "This is where my heart is."

Lupe couldn't help it. "Well, Mr. Carter's sure isn't." She regretted the words as soon as they left her lips and her hands flew to cover her mouth in embarrassment. The two just stood there for a second, and then they both started to laugh, trying and failing to hold it back. God, they were terrible! But just thinking that made her laugh harder.

"Torres!" her uncle barked from behind Lupe and the laughter left them in a whoosh. She and Hernán nodded to each other with sneaky smiles, then turned around to face the chief.

"Sorry to break up the fun, but officer Torres and I have work to do. Come on, young man. Let's walk the perimeter of the crime scene and see how much you know about policing." Then he pointed to Lupe, who was stifling a yawn. "And you, go back to bed. You're only causing trouble here."

Lupe made her face serious and saluted him, and gratefully started back to the condo. In her mind, she was already crawling under the crisp sheets.

It was mid-morning by the time she heard her uncle's key in the condo front door, but she swung it open before he could even turn it. She stood there, one hand on her hip in frustration.

"I've been texting you! You couldn't take two minutes to text me back? I've been worried to death!"

Her uncle lifted his head and looked around the room. "¿Mami? Is that you? Are you back from the dead?"

A smile lifted one side of Lupe's mouth but she quickly adjusted it so she looked serious. "Very funny. But you could have answered."

Esteban lowered himself into the cane rocking chair in the sitting room with a contented groan. "Ah, because I'm such a texter, right? Did you even go back to sleep?"

"Yeah, but when I woke up and you weren't back, I got worried." Lupe sat down on the chair next to him. "Well? What did you find out? Any idea who killed him?"

"Ay, Lupe, it could have been anyone. I've never encountered someone who was so universally detested by his community. But several of his neighbors say they saw what they thought were fantasmas last night, walking around the streets."

Lupe's heart quickened. "The ghosts? Really?"

Her uncle nodded, then leaned his head against the cushioned back of the chair and closed his eyes.

Her mind reeled as she remembered their faces as they reached for her. It was time to tell her uncle about what happened to her and Javier on the beach.

"Tío, I have to tell you something."

Her uncle said nothing, and she could tell by the rhythmic movement of his chest that he was falling asleep.

"Tío!"

He jumped, his hand reflexively reaching for his sidearm. "What? What's wrong?"

"I have to tell you something!"

"Lupe, I'm so tired. Can we talk in an hour or two?"

"But Javier and I saw the ghosts. And met an old man near the unexploded ordnance beach who thinks he knows who the ghosts are, but he might be too crazy to get an answer out of him, and then—"

She could see he was fully awake now.

"Okay, slow down, sobrina. What did you say about you being on a beach with unexploded ordnance?"

Chapter Eleven

Javier

☠

JAVIER WAS WAITING impatiently outside the town offices when the police cruiser pulled up and Lupe jumped out. When he got her text, he had offered to go to town for needed supplies in order to make this little trip in the middle of his workday and meet her, but if he took too long his boss would be pissed. Bad enough he'd been so tired after the wild picnic dinner with gate-crashing ghosts last night. But Lupe had been all excited when she messaged him, something about the body of an old gringo.

She walked up to him with a big smile on her face and he thought about leaning forward and kissing her, but the policeman in the car was watching him. Besides, he wasn't sure they were still on that kind of standing. Last night hadn't been exactly romantic. She balanced a bit on her toes, and he wondered if she was thinking about the same thing.

"Hey!" Her smile was bright and beaming, and he couldn't help smiling back, despite the crankiness that had been hanging in a thick cloud around his head since he'd opened his eyes earlier that morning.

"Hey."

"Thanks for meeting me," she said with way more enthusiasm than he was capable of at that time of the morning. "Let's go in, I'll explain." As they made their way into the town offices, she filled him in on the events of the night before. So much had happened in the time between when Chachu had dropped them off downtown last night and the morning. Way too much. She told him that they had found the same boot prints on the ground around the old man's house as they had in the mangroves on the edge of the bio bay.

"But what do you think we can find here?" He pointed to the walls of the dirty gray industrial town building they were in. He had to be honest. Though he loved seeing her, Javier's mind was more on not losing his job.

"Turns out the old man, Carter, was very wealthy, owned tons of land, so I want to see if he had something to do with the land grab that the resort did after the hurricane. My uncle called and requested the paperwork related to all of Carter's property over the last twenty years. It's public record, but I didn't think they'd give it to me."

Just the mention of the buying-up of the land while the island was desperately trying to recover started Javier's blood to boiling. And that he was actually working for them? Helping them develop the land they pretty much stole? Well, he worked to live with that every day. He pulled his mind back to the present as his counselor had taught him. If he gave in to the rage, it was so much harder to pull out of it, to bring himself back into his body, and not lash out at anyone who happened to be around.

Lupe stepped up to the counter but before she could say anything, the older woman placed a file in front of her, thick with papers. Lupe just looked at the manila folder in confusion. The woman sighed and said, "Tu eres la sobrina de Esteban Dávila, ¿verdad?"

"Sí. Pero, how did you . . . never mind. Gracias." She gathered the folder and walked over to the uncomfortable-looking chairs in the corner. The smells of cheap coffee and discontent were thick in the air; Javier just loved government offices. They always made him think of *Beetlejuice*. And death.

The minute she sat down, Lupe began shuffling through the papers. Why did she want him along for this? He was not a paper-pushing kind of guy, after all. His phone buzzed. Probably work. He pulled it out and saw another text from Carlos.

Man, u gonna call me back or what? R u ghosting me? I need 2 talk 2 u, 'mano.

Ghosting. If Carlos only knew . . .

Javier put the phone back in his pocket with a grumble. Carlos had been texting and calling him all week, probably something ridiculous about the concert for the opening. Carlos had been hired as the main attraction, since his song "El Cuco" had been an international hit after the "incident" last summer, to the point where people on social media were suggesting they'd staged the showdown with the legendary monster. But Javier was irritated that his friend was doing the concert at all. Wasn't it a public show of support for the developers?

Yeah, he understood how ridiculous that sounded. Who was he to talk? He worked for them too. But he needed the money, Carlos didn't, and jobs were seriously scarce down here these days.

Lupe stood before him and dropped a pile of papers in his lap. "Look at this. Most of that land the resort corporation is building on? It belonged to that old gringo who was killed last night. I can't find a bill of sale, but I have to imagine he sold them most of the land they are building on!"

Javier's jaw tightened as he looked over the documents. She was right. It only made him feel more shame.

She was looking at him with a big smile on her face. He had to admit; the smile bugged him just a bit. He knew that she enjoyed finding clues, solving puzzles, but it bothered him that she was having fun with this. His phone buzzed again. This time it was work. They were looking for the big-ass tub of grout he was supposed to be picking up. As if the patio was the most important thing in the world. He put his phone away with a sigh. "Lupe, I have to get back to work."

She looked up with a distracted expression. "Oh, right. Okay. I'm going to keep digging."

"But how will you get back to the condo? Can your tío get you a ride?"

Just then the door swung open, the heavy morning air riding in on a wave. It was Sam, sans tennis whites this time, wearing a faded pair of expensive jeans and a polo shirt, his hair clearly wet from a shower. He noticed them and gave a small wave. "Hey. What are you two doing here?"

Javier didn't even listen as Lupe explained in a quick, excited voice. He was too busy comparing himself—and losing—to Sam.

"Isn't that great, Javier?"

"Hmm?" Wow, he really hadn't been listening.

"Sam offered to help me with the research."

Oh, great. So, he had to leave his girl with this rich boy digging through dusty files, thighs touching, because he had no choice but to go back to his super-shitty job.

Sam shrugged. "These murders are beginning to freak me out. I mean, those guys weren't friends of mine, but it's creepy. My father is not worried about it, only how it will affect attendance at the opening ceremonies and the bookings for the rest of the summer."

Javier snorted. "Typical."

Lupe gave him the side-eye. "Well, I'm glad for the help. Hey, Sam, do you think I could catch a ride back to my uncle's condo when we're done?"

Javier's stomach dropped.

"Sure! Happy to."

He looked *way* too happy for Javier's taste.

Lupe turned to him. "See you tonight, Javier?"

Javier gave a noncommittal grunt, shoved his hands in his pockets, and left.

Lord, he was being an asshole. He knew it better than anyone, but he didn't seem to have control over it. It was like he could hear a voice in his head telling him to be polite, that he should at least make an effort to be pleasant, supportive company for Lupe, but then he couldn't make the right words come out of his mouth.

As he started up the truck, he remembered that he still had to pick up the supplies that he had offered to get in order to make this little trip.

The day was only getting worse as the minutes ticked on.

Chapter Twelve

Lupe

SAM SAT WITH Lupe for hours, poring over documents. When she was bracing herself to go up again and deal with the disgruntled clerk, she was relieved when he offered to go for her. When he approached the counter with his Crest-bright smile, the older woman beamed at him, called him *Señor*. Seemed rich-boy charm opened doors. Especially since then they were able to get access to information she was certain she would never have been able to see without his pull as the son of the developer. But there was still no bill of sale.

Lupe's mind was drifting as Sam chatted up the woman behind the counter when a door to the back office opened. An older woman came through, shoe-horning a file into her worn tote bag. She had long gray hair held back in a ponytail, and loose cotton clothing in bright colors. She could have walked off the streets of Vermont. As if sensing the eyes on her, she looked up and smiled at Lupe, her lined face kind and sun-baked. Then Sam laughed at something, and the older woman appeared to notice him and stopped short, her eyes narrowing. She waited until Sam turned from the counter, then she stepped up to him.

"You have no right to be here! You and your family!" she yelled at him.

Sam looked stunned, the smile bleeding from his face.

Lupe was never one to sit quietly. She stepped up and stood between them. "And what right do you have to tell him that?" she said, folding her arms across her chest.

The woman pointed a finger at Lupe. "Young lady, I've lived on this island for thirty years, I am part of this community, and I don't appreciate people coming in and taking advantage of my friends and neighbors!"

Lupe just stood there. Hard to argue with that. She was trying to come up with some kind of retort, but she had none.

Sam touched her arm and said, "It's okay, Lupe."

The woman glared at him, then stormed to the front door, yanking it so hard it banged on the inside wall.

As it swung closed, Lupe finally yelled out, "Well . . . who says he's like his father?" But the words were too late and fell to the floor like deflated balloons.

Sam smiled at her and shrugged. "I'm afraid that's something I've had to get used to, given who my father is."

She was about to say something—she knew a lot about disappointing fathers—when Sam switched gears, his face lighting up. "Look at this." He spread a surveyor's map out on the coffee table in front of them, his manicured hands flattening out the rolling edges and placing their phones down to hold the corners. The map was browning at the edges and smelled like wet books, but she was fascinated by the concentric rows of elevation lines that encircled the hilltops like spiderwebs.

Sam pointed to the uppermost left corner of the area shaded as a natural reserve. "My father's resort is here," he said, indicating the land near Isabel Segunda.

"Right . . ." Lupe drew the word out, waiting for the punch line. And why did he feel the need to point this out? Everyone knew he was rich. The six-figure car and perfect teeth were a dead giveaway.

"But look at this. The property goes into this part here." He ran his finger over into the shaded area.

"Wait, they're building on the nature preserve?"

"Right."

"So, that has got to be a violation. . . ."

"Right." He glanced over his shoulder at the desk clerk, who looked about to doze off. Sam spoke in a low voice. "Yeah, but my father has all kinds of political connections. Something like this wouldn't be hard to get *'ignored.'*" He glanced again at the clerk and dropped his voice even further. "We have to go about this carefully."

Lupe stared at him for a bit. "Why?"

"Why? I just told you, he has politicians in his pocket—"

"No, I mean why are you doing this? He's your father." She thought of her own father. He had been a shitty parent, drunk for years, not there for her, but at least he was trying now. She loved him. And he was her father.

"I don't know. He's always put business before his family. And I hate that he gets to do whatever he wants and to hell with the environment, with the people . . . with what his family wants or needs."

She examined him, the perfect boy with the perfect teeth and seemingly perfect life. It's funny that how someone appears on the outside can be the complete opposite of their reality. "I take it you didn't want to come down here?"

He shook his head. "No. I was so angry that they didn't give me a say in the matter. I mean, I'm nineteen, you know? I should have a say in how I spend my summers. But then I . . . met someone. But I can only sneak out to the mainland a couple of times a month, and it's even harder for my . . . friend to get away. And do you know what's worse? Dad isn't even here! He installs me and the family in a house on the hill, then takes off back to the mainland for meetings! It doesn't make any difference to him where we are based."

His blue eyes were so heavy with sadness Lupe's heart broke. "Well, I'm glad you're here now." Lupe put her hand over his. "And I look forward to meeting your 'friend.'"

He smiled and put his other hand over hers, then she put her second hand on his until they had a pile and the laughter rose to such a level that the counter lady gave them a chastising look. Sam pulled his hands away and coughed.

"Okay, so what's our next step?" He smiled. He seemed to be enjoying this.

Lupe shrugged. "I don't have a clue. You?"

Sam pointed to his chest with exaggerated movement. "Moi? Um, rich white boy here, remember? My family is the *subject* of protests, not the initiators."

Lupe smiled. She liked this guy.

"But whatever we're going to do, we'd better do it before the grand opening event."

"What? Why?"

"Because my father has invited a group of possible investors to check out the property and to consider investing in some further projects on the mainland."

"'Further projects?'"

"Yeah." He wiped his hands over his face and Lupe knew something bad was coming. "Lupe, he's looking to privatize the beaches."

"What? No. All beaches on the island are public. Access is the only thing that can be controlled."

"Yes, *now*. But what he's proposing would change that."

"But they can't do that. The Puerto Rican government would never allow it."

"The island is broke! Has been since way before Maria. They don't have a lot of options."

"Jesus." Her head was spinning. What other kinds of horrible things were being planned behind closed doors? "Who knows about this?"

Sam held his hands open as if in surrender. "I don't know. The governor, he'd have to know. Someone in Washington. Pretty high up, I imagine. He has to have gotten those permits through somehow."

"Okay, this is much bigger than I had imagined." Ghosts and monsters she could deal with, but politics? Oh *hell* no. They needed to call in the big guns. "Okay, I know just who to call." She pulled out her phone and pressed Marisol's contact.

Chapter Thirteen

Marisol

💀

MARISOL HAD PRETTY much painted herself into a corner of the roof while rolling on silver sealant when her cell phone rang. It startled her so much, she almost fell onto the newly applied asphalt coating. Who was calling her now? She looked at the screen and smiled. Lupe. Of course. She swiped her newly calloused finger across the phone. "Should have known it was you, nena. Your timing is terrible, as usual." She smiled and stepped carefully over to settle down at the edge of the roof. Perhaps it was a good time for a break. Besides, the view from this perch on a mountainside was a sea of lush green. Shocking how quickly the plant life bounced back after Maria. The only break in the color was the bright blue of the FEMA tarps covering the still leaking—or even missing—roofs of the modest houses in this rural town.

"You in the middle of something, Mari?"

Marisol put her long-handled roller down and lay back on the only dry surface, which was surrounded by chemical-smelling sealant, her legs hanging off the edge of the flat roof. She stretched long, liking the way her body felt so strong now after the last few months of physical labor. She'd learned during the hurricane recovery that you needed strength to deal with times like these. "Not anymore. What's going on? What are you doing on Vieques?"

"You know Tío. Something's come up."

"In Vieques? Nothing comes up in Vieques. It has only one speed, slooooow."

"That's what I hear, but not right now. Did you hear about the murders?"

Marisol sat up straight. "Wait? What murders?" Lord, she thought she'd put this shit behind her. Half the reason she was volunteering miles from San Juan was to take it slower after the insanity of last summer *and* the hurricane.

"Three sons of investors in a resort out here and an old gringo who we think sold them the land to build on after the hurricane."

Marisol took a deep breath. Her counselor was always giving her tools and tricks to control her anger. She exhaled slowly. But none of them seemed to be working right then and there. She had to pick her battles, and they all weren't her battles. Or so she told herself several times a day. "Okay, I'm still not sure why you're calling me. I mean, your uncle—"

Lupe started whispering into the phone, and Marisol wondered where she was in that moment. "And then the developer who's building this gargantuan resort here—the one that Javier's working at—well it seems he's planning to get some investors and buy up the beaches on the mainland and privatize them—"

"What?" No amount of slow breaths could stop the old familiar rage from welling up inside her skull at that. "I thought that was just an internet rumor."

"Doesn't seem to be. I'm calling you because we're not sure what the next step is. I mean, it seems like there's a connection, but it doesn't explain the ghosts."

"Ghosts?" The conversation had become totally surreal. Marisol considered for a moment that maybe she'd actually fallen off the roof and died and this was hell.

"Yeah, ghosts. We're . . . I mean, people are seeing crowds of ghostlike figures walking around the island in vintage clothing."

"You sure it's not just a goth concert?"

"Yeah. I'm sure."

"But you're not certain they're the ones killing people, are you?"

"How do you do that?"

"Do what?"

"Know what I'm thinking before I say it, even over the phone?"

Because in a scary way, we think alike, she thought but did not say aloud.

Lupe continued. "The answer is no; I'm not certain. But the locals seem to be, and they're putting a lot of pressure on my uncle to solve it and get rid of the ghosts. And Sam says we have to figure this out before the grand opening event."

"Wait, who is Sam?"

"Umm, a new friend. He's right here with me."

"A new friend, hmm? So how is this Sam wrapped up in all of this? There's something you're not telling me."

"I promise I'll fill you in when I see you. Do you have any idea for a next step?"

"I do, but you're not going to like it."

"I'm not liking much of anything about this trip so far."

"Hmm. Okay, put a bookmark in that thought for when we see each other. But I think we should go see Professor Quiñones."

"Ugh. Isn't there someone else we can talk to? The man doesn't care for me."

"No. He's the expert on folklore and stories of the island, and you know that."

"I guess so."

"Okay, so you want to meet tomorrow at the university?"

"Sure."

"Don't sound *too* excited, Lupe."

"Sorry. Thank you for being willing to help. I'm just . . . struggling this time."

"Yes, we'll talk about that when we see each other."

"Okay, hasta mañana."

Marisol stood up on the roof and grabbed her roller. She was almost done, and then this new roof would be sealed, heat-reflective, and waterproof. Maybe after that there was some demolition that needed doing. After hearing all that she wanted to break something. She had felt so good, gotten several dozen more signatures on her petition from the volunteers before she started working, but now? If she was supposed to choose her battles, there wouldn't be any more important than this one. And she had to admit, it had her name written all over it.

Marisol got to the campus early and sat down on the pink stone steps to wait for Lupe. The late morning sun was golden and warm, the stone of the steps cool and smooth. She leaned back against her favorite column, the one that featured a cameo carving of Lady Justice with her sword and scales. Marisol's mother used to take her to this campus when she was little, and she always went straight for this image and ran her fingers over the carving and imagined herself as this Roman goddess of justice. She had even wanted to dress as her for Halloween one year, but her mother hadn't liked the idea of her wandering around blindfolded. She never *did* get to have any fun.

"Mari!" And there was Lupe, with her Vermont-snow-white skin and bouncy walk. If you were going to go to central casting for "Marisol's friend" this was not who you would pick. But somehow, they worked together. This Gringa-Rican was fierce, and Marisol liked that in a friend.

"What's up, chica?" They hugged tightly. Marisol was not the hugging type, but for this girl she made an exception. Actually, she didn't really have a choice. "Oh, that's right, what's up with you is the usual monsters and mayhem, right?"

Lupe smiled. "Yeah, but not by choice. One summer I'd like to come down here and have, like, a normal vacation."

Marisol shook her head. "I'm sorry, I have no clue what that would look like."

"Yeah, I can only guess from stereotypical hearsay, but I'm thinking sitting on the beach, drinking frozen concoctions, looking at cute boys . . . or did I just steal that from a teen novel?"

"You might have, but I gotta admit, it sounds appealing right now."

After walking for a while in silence, Marisol realized Lupe was staring at her with a smile on her face.

"What?" she barked.

Lupe's smile grew. "Nothing, you just look so . . . strong."

Marisol was horrified to feel the heat behind her face. Truth was, she liked it. "Is that a compliment, or judgment?" she joked, though she knew it was a compliment.

"A compliment, you jerk!" Lupe pushed her gently, teasingly. "I'd kill for arms like those."

They started walking into the main clocktower building of the University of Puerto Rico, and it struck Marisol that even though they hadn't seen each other for months, she felt comfortable with Lupe. Something she didn't often feel. They were early for their appointment, so they strolled down the walkway that led behind the building. The scrappy paths were lined by stunted palm trees, their trucks bent and chewed, all leaning in one direction as if listening, leaves and branches stolen in a hurricane's breath.

Lupe tilted her head back, eyes closed, and not for the first time Marisol wondered what it was like to live in a place like Vermont with so little sun. As they walked, Lupe asked, "How is the rebuilding going?"

Marisol sighed. "So slow. Painfully slow. And there's no money coming from the States at this point. But we're doing what we can."

"Does everyone have power by now?"

"Most areas. Of course, it's the poorer towns that still don't have it back."

Lupe scoffed. "So infuriating." She looked at her watch and without a word they both started back toward the building and up the stairs to the second floor and the faculty offices.

"But we're helping to do repairs to homes, clearing roads. Whatever we can do."

Lupe stopped walking and turned to face Marisol. "Thank you."

"What are you thanking me for?"

"For all the work you're doing for other people."

Marisol started to feel uncomfortable. Lupe's overexpression of emotions was a lot to get used to. "Dávila, don't get all mushy on me. Besides . . ." She pointed to the door they were standing in front of. "You have to prepare to get lambasted by . . . what do you call him?"

"Professor Cranky Pants."

"Oh yes, now I remember. So mature."

Lupe stuck her tongue out at Marisol and rested her knuckles on the door. "So, let's get this over with, shall we?" She knocked three times, quick and sharp.

Almost immediately a handsome, lean guy in his mid-twenties—a graduate student, perhaps?—opened the door and pulled them in. "Come in, quickly, he's waiting for you." Then he whispered, "I think he forgot to take his meds this morning."

"Oh, joy," Lupe added as they were ushered to the inner room, the sanctum of Professor Quiñones. Marisol had met the professor before, at an academic event at the Institute of Puerto Rican Culture, but she'd never been to his office. Of course, Lupe had, and she doubted he'd forgotten *that* visit. To say that her friend and the professor had not gotten along was a huge understatement.

As they walked through the first room, hundreds of saint statues glared at them, their eyes seeming to follow each step, and Marisol wondered if they were plotting their demise. She whispered to Lupe, "I bet if you slept in here these things would come alive and kill you in your sleep."

"Trust me, there's no way anyone could relax enough in here to fall asleep."

And as if on cue, a craggy voice reached them from behind the large wooden desk. "Well? Are you coming in or not, young ladies? I don't have time to waste, I'm an old man, you know!"

Marisol knew from experience that the old cranky ones lived forever. When they went to visit her great-grandmother, she was still bellowing at them from her rocking chair, her gnarled index finger pointed at Marisol in disapproval. And the last time Marisol had seen the professor, he'd been the exact same way. It had only been about a year and a half since she'd last seen the professor, but he seemed . . . diminished, somehow. His already pale skin was even whiter, with blue veins running across his temples like a road map.

Marisol stepped forward, since Lupe had told her how badly her last meeting with the man had gone. "Professor, I don't know if you remember me, but we met at the Institute—"

He looked at her with almost a smile. Almost. "Of course, I remember you. The lecture about the African influence on island poetics. You asked pointed and well-thought-out questions about the whitewashing of Luis Palés Matos."

Marisol gaped at him. There was no faulting the man's memory.

"You're surprised I remembered at my age, yes?"

She nodded, then quickly shook her head. "No, I mean not at your age, but you must meet dozens of people at each event. And I'm only a high school student."

He stood up then, as if he had been inflated. "Ah, but that's precisely why I remember you." He walked around the desk to stand in front of her. "Your line of inquiry was controversial, of course, but that you were asking the questions that the more 'mature' scholars in the room didn't dare to ask was what stuck in my memory."

Marisol was still gaping. She was used to being pushed off, ignored. "I . . . I appreciate your kind words, Professor."

He dismissed her with a wave. "Bah! Nothing kind about them. Just the truth." Then he walked over to Lupe. "Now this one I remember clearly as well. The sharp-tongued gringa. It seems my information proved helpful in your El Cuco exploits, hmm?" He pointed to a series of framed newspaper articles about El Cuco—which included interviews with the cranky academic, of course. A lopsided smile lifted the wrinkles on one side of his face, and Lupe seemed to shrink slightly in front of him. Only slightly.

"Yes. Thank you."

Knowing Lupe, Marisol bet that hurt to say.

Quiñones held his hand to his ear as if listening harder. "I'm sorry, I didn't catch that. Old-man hearing, you know." The smile lifted even higher.

Lupe stood taller and practically shouted, "Yes, thank you, sir. For your kind and knowledgeable assistance!"

The old man stood to his full height, which was formidable, and said, "Ah, now, that wasn't too painful, was it?"

"Actually, it kind of was." Lupe's eyes narrowed and Marisol figured she'd better get right to it before her friend threw a punch.

"Professor, we're looking to get your thoughts on a situation in Vieques. Have you heard about the recent murders?"

"My dear, I'm a cultural anthropologist, it is my job to know what is going on in today's world."

Marisol held her tongue. She needed to get to the point before she held him down so Lupe *could* hit him. "Professor, have you heard of any stories about ghostly figures walking around on Vieques?"

That got his attention. "Well of course, but I haven't heard of any occurrences of that sort since . . . well, since 2001." He moved quickly, much faster than she expected him to, and keenly pulled a notebook of articles off a seemingly disorganized bookshelf.

"When the navy was there?"

He just smiled at that with a cat-that-ate-the-canary look. What was he holding back? He ignored her question and continued, without any hurry, until he found the place in the notebook he was looking for and set it down on the desk open to certain articles. "Yes, the ghosts were wearing period dress, if I remember correctly."

Lupe stared at him, then at the notebook. "How did you know that? That wasn't in any of the articles I read."

"My dear, if my work was limited by what those idiots printed in the newspapers, I would be bagging groceries in Amigo by now."

Oh no he didn't. Heat started to rise behind Marisol's face. But Lupe's tongue was quicker.

"Is there something wrong with bagging groceries, Professor?" Lupe was squaring her shoulders, ready for a throwdown. Marisol looked at her and they locked eyes, anger coming off both of them like static. Damn classist a-hole. Then, in that moment, Marisol took a slow breath in and shook her head slightly, and Lupe paused, then gave a slight nod in response. Silently they agreed this was not today's fight.

"Doctor Quiñones." Using his official title was sure to get him back on track; classist a-holes loved their titles. "We would greatly appreciate it if you would share any thoughts or information you have on this phenomenon."

He straightened his too-loose suit coat and moved behind his desk to sit in the leather chair. Then he tented his fingers in front of him. "Of course, of course. The first references to the appearance of ghosts on the little island were in the late 1920s and early 1930s. Of course, their dress was not considered antiquated then."

Lupe stepped closer. "So, you're saying the clothes they are wearing are from that time period?"

"Precisely." He opened a desk drawer with a resounding squeal, then pulled a worn, overstuffed manila folder from its depths. "Yes, here it is." He pulled out a sheet of paper that was thick and yellowing, with a line drawing on the front. "This is an artist's rendering from Isabel Segunda in the early 1930s." He laid the thick page on the desk and turned it around so it faced the girls. "This is the first example I found from the documentation at the time. This artist was from Vieques and his subjects were often anticolonialist."

They both leaned over to examine the artwork and Marisol asked, "What is the title? I can't quite make it out."

He put a pair of thin reading glasses on the tip of his nose and read, "*Titi Margaret returns to fight.*"

Marisol straightened up. "To fight what?"

But the professor was staring at Lupe. Marisol looked over

and saw that her friend was staring at the illustration, chewing on her lip, her eyes wide.

The professor asked in the gentlest voice he'd managed yet, "Miss Dávila? I'm getting the sense that this time you've seen the supernatural phenomenon yourself, am I right?"

Lupe just nodded.

Marisol stared at her. "What? You didn't tell me that!"

But Lupe didn't respond to that, just grimaced a bit and stood taller. "So, let's say I have, what do you think they want when they appear?"

"Once again you search for the want. Always looking for justifications. Why can't they just exist?"

"But they appear at particular times. I would imagine there is a purpose to the 'when' if not the 'why.'"

"Ah, now that's a different query than your original one. Yes, the 'why' is interesting. So, you're saying they are back, and people are seeing them now?"

"Yes."

"Are they causing any harm?"

"Four people have died since they were first seen. Their hearts were removed from their bodies."

He looked at Lupe in that discerning way he had, bushy white eyebrows raised. "Do you think these ghosts are committing these ghoulish acts?"

Lupe looked nervous. "Well, when I saw the ghosts, one of them, a woman, was reaching for my chest, like she wanted something."

He looked at her without saying anything for some time, then said, "That must have been terrifying."

Lupe swallowed, her eyes glassy. "It was."

He sank back into his chair, tired lines deepening on his face. "Well, I've never heard of ghosts that could make physical contact to the point of evisceration."

Lupe perked up. "That's true! They didn't even leave foot-steps in the sand!"

Marisol's mind was clicking. "Lupe, I think we should look into who has the most to gain from the deaths of the individual victims. And how it might be connected to when the sightings originally happened, around . . ." She pulled the drawing closer to her and peered at the signature again. "Nineteen thirty."

Lupe continued talking as if in a trance. "The resort they're building. It's on land that's supposed to be saved as a nature preserve."

The old scholar barked, "It was supposed to belong to the people who owned it in 1941 when the navy 'relocated' them." He did air quotes with his long, bony fingers.

"Wait, what do mean? Relocated them to where?"

"St. Croix, mostly. Three thousand people, if I remember correctly. Mostly farmers. And the land they moved them to was barren."

Marisol froze. "Wait, St. Croix? What was it Abuelita said . . ." The other two were asking her questions, but Marisol was lost in her own head. "She was angry that 'they made us leave . . . left her there alone.'"

Lupe threw up her hands. "Left who alone?"

"Abuelita," Marisol said absently. Then she realized no one else was talking, and she saw Lupe and the professor gawping at her. "It was just, there's this old woman at a shelter in Yabucoa. She said her grandmother was on Vieques and she was angry they 'made us leave.'"

A loud sigh brought Marisol's attention back to the present, and she and Lupe looked over at the professor.

It was as if he had deflated into his chair, a clockwork man wound down. "This is all so very compelling, children, but you're going to have to find the rest of these answers on your own." He shoved the papers back into their folder and dropped it on his desk as if exhausted just from holding it. "Now if you'll excuse me, I need to rest before my afternoon lecture."

Lupe looked like she was about to push further, so Marisol grabbed her by the arm and pulled her toward the door that led to the outer office. "Of course, Professor. Thank you for your time." Lupe allowed herself to be dragged past the assistant and out into the hall, the door clicking shut behind them.

Marisol let go of her upper arm. Damn. She should have gotten his signature on the petition.

"Well, that went about as well as last time. I just love that man," Lupe said, rubbing her upper arm.

"I liked him."

Lupe looked at her with a sardonic smile. "You would! He was warmer to you than I thought the old crow was capable of."

Marisol smiled back. "I think you don't get along because you two are just too damn alike." She started walking to the stairs with Lupe following behind.

"What? Now see here, young lady! I didn't attain three Oxford degrees so that I could sit here and listen to a child babble!"

"See, now you've gone and taken it too far."

"Two Oxford, one Harvard?"

"Nah, 'child babble'? That was plain lazy."

Chapter Fourteen

Lupe

💀

SHE'D RIDDEN OVER from the ferry to Río Piedras with her uncle, but he had to return to Vieques earlier, so Marisol dropped Lupe off at the late afternoon ferry, the sun melting Creamsicle orange across the top of the ocean. Marisol was going to join her the following day after she stopped at home and packed a few things for crashing at Lupe's uncle's condo. As Lupe walked away, Marisol was sitting in her car tooling around on her phone, waiting to make sure Lupe got on the ferry, when she called out the open window. "Hey, Lupe."

Lupe turned around. "What? Miss me already?"

Marisol smiled. "No, next time you put some shit like that on your Facebook page, add a trigger warning or something."

Huh? "What are you talking about? I forgot I even have a page. Facebook's for old people." She started walking back to the car, a weird feeling roiling in her belly. She got to the window and looked down at Mari's phone.

Marisol scrolled until the picture of a heart was revealed, a real heart, a trickle of blood spilling onto the sand, the flesh of the organ glistening in what looked like early morning sunlight.

"What the hell?"

Marisol scrolled a bit. "There's a caption."

Picture yours here.

Lupe took the phone from Marisol so she could look closer, her stomach in full roil now. "This makes no sense; the post says it's from me. I must have been hacked." She handed the phone back.

Marisol gaped at her. "You're not concerned about this?"

"Look, it's probably some kid trying to scare me."

Marisol lowered her gaze. "With a photo of a bloody human heart on a beach? Pretty elaborate for a 'kid.'"

Lupe shrugged, but began chewing on her lip.

"Lupe, this is on Vieques."

"What?"

She pointed to the photo. "Even though this was at night, I can see the white balustrades of the seawall in Esperanza, here."

Lupe shrugged again, this time with less enthusiasm. "Could be a coincidence."

Marisol got out of the car at that one. "Someone or something is tearing the hearts from people on a tiny island—that tiny island"—she pointed across the water—"right over there, your uncle is investigating it, you're asking questions, and someone posts a photo of a human heart on your Facebook page taken on the same tiny island the day after one of the murders, and you're saying it could be a coincidence?"

"Okay, when you put it like that . . ."

Marisol grabbed Lupe by the shoulders. "Girl, you have to tell your uncle."

"No!" She pulled out her phone, opened her Facebook app, and deleted the post, then looked into deleting her account. "No. If we tell him he'll just send me back to San Juan under house arrest, or worse, back home to Vermont."

"Maybe that's not a bad idea."

Lupe's eyes shot up from her phone.

"I mean, I want to see you. We all want to see you, but I think everyone would rather you stay safe."

Lupe was shaking her head so hard her eyeballs shook. "No way. I'm staying. I'm in the middle of this, and I'm going to help sort it out. Besides, I have to figure out what's going on with Javier."

"Yeah, we didn't get to talk about that."

"Nothing to talk about, really. I need him to talk."

"Are you sure it's just him?"

"What's that supposed to mean?"

"I mean, I've been wondering what's going on in your life for the last six months, but all we've talked about is the hurricane, my work, my family, not yours."

Lupe put her hands on her hips. "Yeah, well, a category-five hurricane in your homeland kind of takes precedence over track meets and pre-college courses."

"No! It doesn't! See, I want to know about your athletics and your classes. It makes the nightmare here feel better, like it can be overcome."

Lupe gave her the side-eye.

"No, really. I want to know that life goes on. Normal life. Maybe Javier did, too."

"I told him things . . . I think." But she couldn't remember any one thing. Hours of conversations about power, and water, and procuring gas. About joining his mother, who was alone in her house in Amapola, her uncle collecting them both and putting them up in his house, no questions asked. About how the community rallied. Lupe did brush off questions about her own life; they seemed so insignificant, but that didn't increase the distance . . . did it?

"Don't think about it now. You did nothing wrong, it's just . . . friendship is both ways. Take it from someone who knows, you can't always be giving."

Lupe nodded, but her mind was swirling, rewinding conversations, trying to find a bit of herself in them, but coming up empty.

A ferry horn blew.

"Shit! I gotta go." She pulled Mari into a hug and turned to run to the ferry.

"Think about telling Tío about the Facebook post, Lupe!"

Lupe turned around and smiled as she ran. "What Facebook post?" Okay, this was just an act for her friend's benefit; in truth, Lupe was creeped out.

Lupe loved the feeling of the salt spray across her face, the rock and sway of the aging boat. Considering she had grown up in a landlocked part of the world, she certainly felt comfortable bouncing across the top of the water. She might not have gotten the melanin from her Puerto Rican side, but she sure inherited a love of the sea.

Okay, so the thought of the creepy heart post took away from the scenery, but she refused to let it freak her out completely.

She stepped off the boat's gangplank onto the weathered dock and saw the expected cruiser waiting for her. Or, rather, everyone saw *and* noticed it. She'd probably still prefer an Uber, but as she got to know the individual officers, and with all the help they'd given her the year before, the cruisers were becoming a familiar and comforting sight.

She slipped into the front seat, as was her habit—though it was against the rules, they all made an exception for her— but was surprised to see Captain Torres scowling at her from behind the wheel. "Oh. Hi. I was expecting—"

"Your uncle was occupied so I offered to pick you up, Señorita Dávila."

An insincere smile snaked its way across his face. It was the smile of someone who knew something you didn't and felt pretty damn superior about it. It was her least favorite kind of smile. "Okay . . ." The word was stretched out as she pulled the door closed and buckled herself in. Though she was usually insistent on not sitting in the back like a perp, she wished she were there in that moment. The man gave her the creeps.

He checked the ferry pick-up traffic and pulled out in front of a sedan as if his car was the only priority. "I offered because I wanted to have a little chat with you."

Oh, great. She didn't say anything, just looked out the window as if the dock area was endlessly fascinating.

"I've heard that you and that Sam boy have been . . . inquiring about things related to the town and the resort."

The clerk at the town office. Must have been her. *Note to self: trust no one.* She still said nothing, an unusual thing for her, but she felt it was the best course of action in this situation. She was counting the blocks to the condo, it wasn't far, but the image of the deep red heart on the night beach made her nervous. This was one of the most frightening car rides of her seventeen years, and she had an only-recently-sobered-up father who used to drive her around in his powerful truck after consuming half a bottle of rum. This man made her really uncomfortable. Wait . . . was she riding with a murderer? She knew of one way to find out.

"So, Captain . . . are you on Facebook?" Not subtle, but she was not thinking overly clearly at the moment.

"What? No, I don't have time to waste on social media. That is a game for the young. And, speaking of which, I think it best if you focused on things more appropriate to a teenage girl on vacation."

That snapped her head around. "And what, pray tell, do you think is 'appropriate' for me to be focused on?"

Condescension dripped off his smile. "Oh, shopping, movies, boys, maybe tanning at the beach?" He looked over at her bare legs in a way that made her lunch push against her throat. "And you could certainly use some color, Lupe."

She pulled her shorts down as much as the cotton fabric would allow. "Yeah, not all young *women* are interested in the same things, Captain. And I prefer you call me Señorita Dávila."

He jerked on the steering wheel and turned down a side street she wasn't familiar with. Her skin started to feel tighter. "This is not the way to the condo," she said, and wondered once again if her comments were wisely chosen.

"Well, you don't know everything about this island, do you, *Señorita Dávila*?" His movements were becoming sharper, anger adding edges to each turn of his head, white to his knuckles gripping the steering wheel. Then he slammed on the brakes and she was thrown forward, reaching out to brace herself against the dashboard.

"What the actual f—"

He wheeled around. "Keep your foul mouth shut! You have no right digging into things you can't possibly understand. You and that spoiled rich brat will keep your noses out of the business of this island, comprendes?"

"Are you threatening me, Captain?" Her muscles were taut with fear and ready to run, but unless ghosts were coming (been there, done that) she wasn't a runner. He might not have posted that picture, but he was threatening her, nonetheless.

His lips stretched into a thin line and she imagined the foul things that wanted to make their way out of his mouth. But she watched him suck back his anger and swallow it, and she could tell it tasted bitter. "Mind your own business and we will have no further problems."

She looked at the sparse and seemingly abandoned street, the only sign of life a stray dog who regarded them with hope and visible ribs. There was so much she wanted to say, to ask about what he had to hide—and if he had nothing to hide, why did he care? Then her self-preservation kicked in—was Marisol right? was there someone out to get her, after all?—so she responded "Fine," and wondered if she could get her cell phone out without him noticing.

He pulled into a driveway, grass growing up from between tectonic plates of asphalt, and backed into the street, his hairy arm reaching over the back of her seat as he ignored the backup camera and looked around, old-school style.

She let out a long breath as they pulled back onto the main drag. The few blocks to the condo seemed to go on for miles and miles, but finally he pulled up in front of the building. She was reaching for the door handle before the car came to a complete stop, but he grabbed her upper arm before she could jump out. She looked down at his sausage fingers and then at his face as if she could shoot lasers from her eyes.

"If you tell your tío about our little talk, I'll deny it ever took place."

She narrowed her eyes. "He'll believe me." Her voice was slow and even. "He always does." She wasn't sure of much, but she was sure about her uncle.

"It doesn't matter. He should be worrying about his own job, anyway." And a smile snaked up his face again.

"What is *that* supposed to mean?" She hated that the question shot out so quickly. It was like giving this man something to bite, but she couldn't help it.

He just laughed and let go of her arm.

Though she wanted to ask more, to make him answer, her instincts kicked in again and she slipped out of the car. As she watched the cruiser drive off, she rubbed at her arm and the red marks his fingers left there and wondered what that nasty little man had meant about her tío's job and what it was that he was so anxious to hide.

Chapter Fifteen

Esperanza, Vieques

CHARLIE MURPHY STUMBLED off the main drag of Esperanza, the small town where he was staying on the south of Vieques. It was well past midnight and most of the houses were dark. He liked walking around at that hour. Fewer humans with tiny, boring lives who he had to pretend to give a shit about.

The asshole bartender at his regular hangout had shut him off around ten. He spent the last few hours drinking with the local guys in a kiosk near the beach. It was a dump, but at least it was cheap. He was going to have to find a decent place to—

Wait, did he hear something? He jolted to a stop and listened.

Wind in the trees.

A car revving its engine a few blocks away.

Music pouring from the overpriced restaurant on the corner.

Nothing. He was imagining things.

He wheeled back around, and as he started to walk again his feet tangled. Before he knew it, he was heading toward the ground, face-first. The pavement slammed into him, the impact shuddering throughout his body. That was going to leave a mark. He lay there for a moment, as if he were stretched out on the couch in his apartment, and stared at the loose pebbles peppering the asphalt of Calle Tintillos. He could kind of imagine them as mountains, and he was a giant about to crush them all.

Maybe he'd had too much rum at the bar.

He slowly got to his knees, stopping for a second when the block started to spin, and then brushed off stones that had become embedded in his forearms. Long drips of blood trailed down his pale arms and soaked into the hems of the short sleeves of his crisp white guayabera shirt.

"Shit." He stood, weaving, and brushed off the knees of his khakis. Good thing he wasn't one of those douchebags who wore cargo shorts like they were on goddamn safaris or something. He stood for a minute and lit a cigarette, the lighter's flame glowing unnaturally orange in the heavy night air. Lord, summers were hot on this godforsaken island. But six more months, tops, and he'd be out of there. Six months and another cool million in profits. He smiled to himself as he resumed walking, looking more carefully at the street beneath him.

It was hard to believe he'd been there for only nine months. It felt like an eternity. The winter had been okay. He'd come down as soon as the flights had been reinstated after the hurricane. He went where the money was, and that meant jumping right on it before everything settled down. Take advantage of the chaos, he liked to say. If he were going to write a business book, that would be the title. Yeah, he liked that. Wait! *Ride the Chaos*?

He'd come up with a title later.

He turned the corner onto his street, Calle Magnolia. He couldn't wait to fall into his bed in his blissfully air-conditioned bedroom. When the power was out and kept going out, he had been miserable. His skin would get burnt to hell during the day and he would want nothing but to lie in front of a fan, but no power. The mainland got power back on way before

Vieques, and though that pissed him off, it only made his fundraising more effective. "Help the tiny island of Vieques recover from the devastation of Maria!" He posted photos he'd taken of downed trees and strangers working on repairs as if they were being funded by his "organization." His loud laughter echoed off the buildings on his short street. Screw his neighbors if he woke them up. He wouldn't have to put up with them much longer.

He'd gone out to celebrate. His website had taken in a daily high of almost ten thousand dollars, thanks to some idiot, guilt-ridden, wealthy housewife from Des Moines and a photo of a stray dog with big eyes. Little did she know he'd kicked the mutt right after he'd snapped the photo. But she wanted to "help the dear animals who were left homeless after the hurricane." People were so damn gullible. Few more days like that and he'd get to head back to the States sooner rather than later. If he had to eat any more damn fried plantain, he was going to kill someone. What he wouldn't give for a plain old American steak or decent New York pizza.

A skittering sound echoed behind him and he whirled around again, this time taking care not to fall.

"Wha waz dat?" he slurred, squinting into the dark corners of the street.

Probably Ms. Vasquez's scrawny cat.

God, he hated that thing.

He'd poisoned two of her other cats, but this one was too damn wily and wouldn't take the food he tried to give it.

Oh well, he was almost home. Soon they could all kiss his lily-white, wealthy ass. He turned onto the walkway of his little rented house and tried the front door. Locked. Shit. The cleaning lady must have locked it. He felt in his pockets for his key, but nothing. He always left the back door open. He spun around and leaned his hand on the side of the building as he walked. The ground was tipping a bit. He hated when it did that. The backyard was pitch black, the stars the only source of light overhead. He stopped to take a breather. Boy, he was more tired than he thought.

Another sound came from around the side of the house. Damn cat! He picked up a rock that edged the decorative garden the owner had wasted money on and turned toward where the noise had come from. He was going to bash that little shit's head in once and for all and bury it in this ridiculous garden.

He put his back against the building and edged his way to the corner. He peeked around but couldn't see the cat. All the movement was making him feel queasy, and the greasy mofongo he'd had for dinner pushed up his throat.

To hell with the cat. He dropped the rock and lurched to throw up on the nearest gardenia bush. He could taste the acidic edge of cheap rum on the back of his tongue. Next time he was going to spring for the good stuff. He stood there for a few minutes, hands on his knees, wiping his mouth. When he was sure he was done, he slowly raised himself up to standing. His stomach lurched again. He just needed to make it inside and fall onto his bed. He wouldn't even take off his clothes.

He stood for a second to let the earth stop its weaving and saw a shadow pass behind him.

That was no cat.

"Who's there?" he yelled. Damned if he was going to let some punk take his hard-earned money. He grabbed the pinwheel garden stake—why did anyone waste their money on such shit?—pulled off the shiny metallic top, and turned it over to its business end. The stake was pointy enough. He whipped around, wielding it like Excalibur, swinging it wildly in the air.

"Come out, you coward!" He spun again, and then felt another wave of sickness wash over him. He was bent over once more, thinking he was going to be sick, when the rock hit his skull with a dull *thunk*. As he fell onto the garden's packed earth with its covering of white decorative rocks, his last thought was "God, I hate this garden."

Chapter Sixteen

Javier

💀

JAVIER WAS DREAMING about the hurricane. He was standing on a sidewalk in his hometown of Amapola, and the storm came and lifted him up off the ground, tumbling him out of control and over the city, rain pelting him in the face like bullets, the roar of the wind like a train coming straight for him. He was flailing, trying to right himself as he spun, and someone was holding his hands. Nothing frightened him as much as not having control over his own body. He started to scream and thrash.

"Javi! Stop, man! It's me!"

His eyes shot open and he saw his friend Carlos's face right in front of his. He looked around wildly, trying to get his bearings, and recognized the sad little room the resort had rented for him to stay in during the week while he was working on Vieques. His breathing slowly returned to normal. He looked down at his hands, and Carlos still had them clutched in his. He must have given him a look, because Carlos dropped them and put his own hands up like he was surrendering.

"Sorry, man, but I gave you a shake, and you started punching me. You wouldn't wake up."

Javier rubbed his hands over his face and into his hair, the long curls reminding him that he was overdue for a haircut. "I was having a nightmare. About a hurricane."

Carlos sat back with a sigh. "Most Puerto Ricans are these days."

Javier's mind began to clear. He took a good look at Carlos and saw that he was in full Papi Gringo star gear. Leather jacket, gold chains, sunglasses as dark as midnight. "Wait, what are you doing here?"

"Well, when a brother won't answer your phone calls or call you back, you have to resort to desperate measures."

Javier just stared at him. Was he making any sense?

"Jesus, Javi." He threw his hands up in exasperation. "The concert? The grand opening?"

How long had he slept for? "But that's not till Friday."

"Rehearsal? Sound check? Any of this familiar?"

Javier always had trouble rectifying the image of his childhood friend, goofball Carlos, with the strutting reggaeton star Papi Gringo he had become. It all seemed like he was playing dress-up or something, but since he had an internationally best-selling record it clearly was real to a hell of a lot of people. "Sorry. Things have been kind of wild here."

"Yeah, I heard. My manager wanted me to cancel. He was worried about my safety. Ha! After being five feet from El Cuco this is nothing, ¿verdad?" He put up his fist for a dap.

Javi smiled and pressed his fist against Carlos's and they were kids again. "What have you been trying to reach me about?"

"Don't you want to go back to sleep? We can talk in the morning. . . ."

"Yeah, I don't think that's gonna happen now." He pulled the T-shirt from last night over his head and turned on the lamp on the night table. Now that Carlos was there, in front of him, he felt bad for ghosting him. "It's been weird, man, being around all these murders again. I mean, what are the odds, right?"

"I don't know, bad luck seems to follow us around like a lost dog."

"Not you, 'mano! Your song is an international hit! I saw your sorry ass on the Grammys!"

Carlos smiled. "It was a trip, Javi. I mean, I got pretty big here, you know? But that's a whole nother scale."

"Pretty much a dream come true, ¿verdad?"

"I guess."

"You guess?"

Carlos took off his dark sunglasses. "It's just ... when you're playing on a field that size, you're not calling the shots anymore. The record company won't let me do anything different. I want to try some different kinds of music, stretch different creative muscles ... but they made a shitload of money from the *El Cuco* album and now they want me to just pump out more of the same shit."

"But it was your writing that made the album so good. Can't they trust your instincts?"

"Nah, they keep talking to me about the 'Papi Gringo brand,' like that's someone else. It's like I've created a monster."

Javier gave him a look. "No, man, no more monsters."

Carlos smiled, but it had a touch of sadness around the eyes.

Javier looked at his friend for a bit. He'd never thought about it that way. He could never do it, he liked his privacy, but he thought Carlos lived for that shit. *Just goes to show you, the grass ain't never greener.* He put his hand on Carlos's shoulder. "I'm just glad you're here now."

"That's why I took this gig. Wanted to get in touch with my roots, have my friends—my real friends—backing me up."

Javier pulled back. "Wait . . . you want me to sing backup?" He put his hand on his chest in mock astonishment. "Damn, don't mind if I do!" He grabbed Carlos's sunglasses, put them on, and started belting out one of Carlos's songs, off-key and loud, holding an imaginary mic in his hands as he rapped and beatboxed badly.

Carlos joined in, doing a call and response as the song crescendoed.

A pounding on the wall from the room next door.

Javier and Carlos froze.

Then they burst out laughing so hard tears rolled down their cheeks and they tried to catch their breath as the banging continued, and it was like they were ten again and Carlos's mom was telling them to go to sleep. Finally, they calmed down, falling back onto the bed and sighing.

"Damn, Javi! Don't quit your day job!"

"Oh, if you only knew how much I want to quit my day job." They lay there for a minute, and the quiet of the house was suddenly very loud. "So, what was it you wanted to tell me?"

Carlos jumped to his feet and started pacing the little room. "Okay, okay. There's just . . . there's something I have to tell you. Something I should have told you, and everyone, a long time ago. . . ."

Javier could see that he was uncharacteristically nervous. Here was a guy who regularly performed in front of thousands and thousands of people. He'd sung his hit on *The Tonight Show*, for God's sake, hung out with Jimmy Fallon. *If he's nervous, it must be bad.* He sat up. "I'm listening."

"Okay, it's just, I've been afraid it will ruin my career." He stopped and gestured wildly. "Javi, this business, it's so damn . . . prescribed."

"What do you mean by that, 'prescribed'?"

"There's a way I'm supposed to act, to dress"—he threw his arms up in the air—"to stand, for God's sake! I can't be myself at all, haven't since . . . well, since we were cangrejos, you feel me?"

Javier smiled at the name of their childhood group. Five friends all born in July, all growing up in the same neighborhood. The crabs, Scorpios. "Those were good days, weren't they?"

Carlos matched his smile as he, too, fell back into those simpler times. "Yeah, man. We could be whoever we were and no one cared."

"Until we turned thirteen and it all went to hell."

"Yeah, I guess there's that. But even then, I had this feeling I was different, you know? Like—"

"You didn't fit in."

Carlos stopped and stared at him. "Right. How did you know that?"

"'Cause I felt the same way."

"Really? But, Javi, you were the leader, the cool one, the one we all wanted to be like."

"Yeah, and look at me now!" He gestured around the tiny room, pointed at his minimal possessions spilling out of a duffel bag. "Years of drug addiction, the boogeyman facing me down, and now! The lap of luxury, working for the enemy for minimum wage." God, it sounded so depressing when he put it like that.

Carlos sat down next to him on the bed. "No, man! But you're free!"

"Free? Free? Carlos, I can't continue in college to get a degree so I can get a real job without money, but I can't get money without taking this shit job because the hurricane wiped out half of any employment that was available to me, and I can't even keep a girlfriend without being an angry dick to her. . . ."

"We talkin' about Lupe?"

"Yeah, man. I'm screwing it all up. I'm just so . . . angry."

"I hear that."

Javier looked over at his friend. Carlos hung his head low, and Javier realized he'd brought yet another person down with his dark thinking. "Forget about that. You came here to tell me something important and I want to hear it."

Carlos stood up again, faced Javier, and took a loud breath. "Okay, Javi, it's like this . . . I'm—"

The door busted open and José, a guy from Humacao who Javier worked with, stuck his head in. "Javier! Man, they found another body!" He was breathing fast like he'd been running. Then José looked over and noticed Carlos. "Holy shit!" He took a step back in apparent shock. José tended toward the dramatic. "Is that Papi Gringo? Like, in the flesh?" His eyes lit up and he held his arms in front of him as if to prevent Carlos from running. "Oh man! I'm a huge fan! Can I, like, have your autograph?"

Despite the Escalade's overpriced shocks, Javier's and Carlos's heads hit the ceiling like a rhythm section due to the hurricane-ravaged dirt roads. For some reason, the thick-necked driver didn't seem to be bouncing as much. Probably from the excessive weight of all the muscle. Javier was not fond of driving around in the flashy SUV, but the body had been found in Esperanza, on the other side of the island, and he wanted to check in with Chief Dávila.

Even in the pre-dawn dark, it wasn't hard to find the crime scene. Police cars were coming and going down the side streets with their ultra-bright flashing blue lights, and people were gathering on corners in small bunches. You could almost follow the direction of the onlookers' glances like a GPS. They had gotten within a block when a uniformed cop stepped in front of the car, hand out in the universal "Stop" gesture. He stepped around the side, hands held at his hips, ready to grab weapons as needed. Javier had been straight for more than three years, but the sight of the midnight-blue uniform still made his palms sweat.

The officer was fit and crisp, and when Javier looked at the smooth walnut skin of his face, he realized he wasn't much older than they were, but that didn't make him any less intimidating. The man gestured impatiently for the driver to roll down the tinted windows, but Carlos pressed the button for his first. At the sound of the back window going down the cop jumped back and reached for his sidearm, until he noticed Carlos with his hands up, saying, "It's okay, officer, I just want to talk to you."

The cop's hand didn't leave his handgun in its holster, but he cautiously peered in. Then Carlos lowered his hands from his face, and recognition lit the policeman's features. His hand came off his gun and a smile spread to his eyes. "¡No me digas! Papi Gringo, in my town?" And with that, the intimidating officer looked like someone you'd see at a club, or a Papi Gringo concert. "Man, what are you doing on Vieques?" He hit his head with his palm as he remembered. "The concert! Right! How could I forget?" He unclipped his phone from his hip and started typing on it. "Man, I gotta get a selfie for my sister! She's never gonna believe—" And then he froze, looked up as if just realizing where he was and what he was doing, clipped the phone back on his hip, and stood up brick-wall straight. "Señor, can I ask what business you have in this location?"

Carlos smiled and removed his sunglasses in such a smooth gesture, Javier could tell it was much practiced. "My friend and I"—he gestured over to Javier—"are here to see Chief Dávila. We've done some . . . work with him in the past."

Again, recognition spread over the man's face. "Yes! Of course. I'm sorry, I should have remembered—"

Carlos dismissed the cop's apologies. "No hay ningún problema, officer."

The man tapped his chest. "Freddy. M-m-my name's Freddy."

"Nice to meet you, Freddy. You can call me Carlos." He held his hand out the window to shake.

Freddy grabbed his hand and shook it with an absent look. "Okay, Carlos." The last word like something he was trying on. He looked at their hands and realized he'd been holding on for too long and pulled his back quickly.

They were both smiling big, but Freddy was beaming. Then he caught himself again and gestured toward the activity. "Please, go ahead. I'll radio the chief to let him know you're coming." Then he pulled the radio from the front of his belt.

"I appreciate it, man, seriously." Carlos looked down at the sunglasses in his hand, then held them out the window. "And please, give these to your sister for me. A small token of thanks."

The cop took a tentative step forward and looked at the proffered eyewear. "Nah, you can't be serious. . . ."

Carlos offered them again. "I'm completely serious, 'mano. I want her to have them."

Freddy reached for them as if afraid the glasses were about to be yanked away. Then he held them as if he'd found the damn holy grail. "Adriana's gonna freak!" He pressed his heart with his other hand. "¡Muchísimas gracias! This means so much."

Carlos held the tips of his fingers together and bowed his head, then tapped the driver gently on the shoulder and they started rolling again. Carlos sat back and Javier looked out the back window to see Freddy smiling and waving like a little kid, the sunglasses still clutched carefully in his hand.

Javier shook his head and smiled. "Man, how do you *do* that?"

Carlos smiled back. "Do what?"

Javier gestured to the back window. "That! You reduced that starched and uptight cop to a giggling fan!"

"He didn't giggle."

"Yes, I do believe he giggled."

Carlos leaned toward the driver. "Theo, did you hear Freddy giggle?"

Theo turned his head slightly. "No, sir, I don't believe I heard a giggle."

"Besides, weren't those glasses expensive?"

Carlos waved him off. "Nah, man. They're my brand!"

Javier smiled and shook his head again.

"Besides, I believe I can write those off on my taxes as a donation to island law enforcement, no? I'll have to inquire of my accountant."

They arrived in the midst of the action, and the mood became way more serious. Theo got out and opened Carlos's door. They both climbed out and Javier looked around for Lupe's uncle, seeing him walking around the corner of a small, neatly kept house across the street. You really couldn't miss him. It wasn't his six-foot-four frame or even his linebacker shoulders, it was more his . . . presence. Javier didn't have a better word for it, but when Esteban Dávila walked into a room, everyone not only looked, but snapped to attention and felt as if they'd done something wrong. As they walked over, Javier could feel all the eyes following them. Well, following Carlos. He wondered what it was like to have to deal with this all the time, to never leave your house without a guy like Theo, to always have to be what people expected you to be. Just thinking about it made Javier's breath speed up with anxiety.

The chief noticed them and changed direction slightly to

meet them. He stepped up and shook Carlos's hand without a smile, but his eyes were softer than they had been a minute before. "Carlos. Good to see you."

"Igualmente, Jefe."

Dávila nodded at Javier. "Utierre."

Javier nodded back, then asked, "Another body?" Conversations with the chief were often in shorthand. Javier liked that.

A nod. "Same M.O. as the others," he said in a low voice. His people were keeping at a distance, but Javier imagined they were wondering why the hell he was consulting with a reggaeton star and a recovering heroin addict.

"Were those . . . glowing figures sighted around here, too?"

"That's what the neighbors are saying, but who knows, could be hysteria at this point. And I can't say I blame them."

Javier nodded again. "What are you thinking, Chief?"

The big man sighed. "I have to admit, once again I agree with Lupe. I believe there are . . . ghosts or zombies of some kind wandering around, but I don't think they're doing this."

"Why not?"

Dávila crossed his arms over his chest, his hand rubbing his chin. "I don't know, gut feeling. And there are too many things that don't fit the supernatural theory: footprints, and in this case a blunt weapon to the head." He waved his hands. "Look, after last year I wouldn't be surprised if it were the ghosts, or whatever they are, but I don't imagine they'd need to hit the guy over the head."

"Then who is taking these people's hearts?" Carlos asked.

"That, son, is the multimillion-dollar question."

A wave of voices reached them, coming from down the street and toward the center of town. All heads turned that way and the noise grew in volume as it got closer.

"What now?" Dávila muttered as a group led by a sturdy

woman in a housedress pushed through and stopped in front of him.

"Esteban Dávila?"

Those two words totally had a third-grade-teacher vibe to them. And the hesitant way the chief answered proved it still worked on him, too.

"Yes? Can I help you?"

The woman put her hands on her ample hips and Javier had to smile: that was totally Lupe's move.

"Why aren't you doing anything about these horrible . . . events?" Bright pink curlers quivered in her hair as she shook her head back and forth, her face pale in the overhead glow of the streetlight.

Dávila gestured around him. "I assure you, Señora, we are all hard at work on that very issue."

A man shouted from a few people back. "These fantasmas are killing people! Just like El Cuco on la Isla Grande!" Grumbling agreement was the reply from the surrounding crowd.

Then another man spoke up. "Ghosts? You people are watching too many movies! There's a serial killer on Vieques and they're"—he pointed to the police around him, including the chief—"not doing anything to protect us!"

A woman yelled from within the crowd, "It doesn't matter, ghosts or a killer, no one is safe!"

A mumble rose, not sounding all that different from the horde of ghosts moaning. Javier shivered.

The chief put his hand out in a calming gesture. "Now, there's no indication that these murders were committed by supernatural forces. If you will just go back to your homes and let us do our jobs, I assure you—"

The third-grade-teacher-woman piped up again. It seemed she considered herself a type of leader of the unruly mob. "How dare you, of all people, say that these ghosts don't exist!"

"Now, I didn't say that, I only said that there's no indication they've hurt anybody—"

"Oh, I'm sure the dead are rising because they heard the mofongo is so good at Bigotes Restaurant!"

There was a responding wave of laughter, but the tension of the group was palpable. It was as if Javier could taste it on his tongue. They were afraid, and he didn't blame them.

"Señores y Señoras." The chief didn't yell it, per se, but it was loud and deep, and everything stopped within a ten-yard radius. "If we are to solve these terrible crimes against your beloved community, you have to leave us to do our work."

Clearly something he'd said before. Everyone sort of looked at each other as if confused, until Dávila barked, "Now!" And they scattered like a flock of chickens, walking determinedly in their different directions.

"Bueno." He turned to Javier and Carlos. "I have to get back to my team. Will you two be around if I need to reach you?"

"Yes," they said at the same time.

"Good." And he was off, yelling orders left and right as he walked.

Carlos watched him go. "Why does that man make me feel guilty even when I haven't done anything?"

"I don't know, man, but I think he makes everyone feel that way."

Carlos shrugged. "Probably a useful skill in his position."

They hadn't gotten very far on the short walk back to the car when Carlos was stopped by a group of literally giggling teens for autographs, so Javier took a deep breath and tried to summon patience. He glanced around, fascinated by the street-long hive of buzzing people—in the middle of the night, no less—when he overheard a couple of uniforms talking as they walked by.

"Some of the guys are saying that Chief's in denial again. That a lot more people are going to be killed by these damned zombies if he doesn't smarten up."

"I don't know about zombies, but I heard that if he doesn't solve this quick, before the whole world is tuning in to this opening, the commissioner and the governor are gonna fire him."

"No shit!"

"Yeah man, he stepped on the wrong political toes on this one."

Then they were out of eavesdropping distance. For a moment, Javier considered following, but Carlos stepped over to him before he could decide.

"Wassup, Javi?"

Yeah, no way to trail two cops discreetly with Papi Gringo along. He thought about finding the chief and telling him directly, but with all that was going on, he figured that was not the best idea and this was not the time. "I've got to find Lupe, fast."

"All right! Are the hermanos cangrejos on another quest?" Carlos rubbed his hands together as if he'd been waiting for this moment.

Javier sighed. "I'm afraid so."

Chapter Seventeen

Lupe

LUPE SIPPED HER coffee as the thin paper cup started to feel flimsy with the heat, and looked up and down the street for what felt like the thousandth time. The sun had just risen and still no sign of Javier and Carlos. She had woken up some kid named José who worked with Javier. He was more excited that "Papi Gringo's in the house!" than he was about giving her any kind of useful information. When she'd woken up before sunrise, she discovered that her uncle had left in the middle of the night again; another body, she imagined. She wasn't sorry she'd missed this one. How did he survive on so little sleep? She'd thrown on whatever clothes she could find, grabbed her backpack, and run over to Javier's boarding house, but she'd been sitting on the front steps for more than an hour.

Another person dead. Probably missing a heart. Jesus.

Was it her? Did she drag this kind of supernatural bad luck behind her like a pesky little sibling? Well, more evil than pesky.

A shiny black SUV was turning the corner, navigating the surface of the moon road. Yeah, only one person on the island could be riding in a vehicle that flashy. She stood and stepped toward the road as they pulled up and the back window glided open to reveal Javier's way-more-than-handsome face.

Damn.

She was mad at him, but he sure was gorgeous.

Carlos's face appeared next to Javier's, dark eyes sparkling, flawless light brown skin glowing, and lips curled in a rockstar smile. He wasn't too shabby either. "Damn, girl! What you doin' up so early?" They spilled out of the car in a cascade of handsome boyness.

"I could ask you two the same thing!"

Carlos stepped in front of Lupe and held his arms out for a hug. "It's not early when you never go to bed! Bring it in, beautiful," he said, and he pulled her into a full hug.

She breathed deep, his scent of expensive spice and lime heady and soothing. Then she held him at arm's length. "Looking good, Papi Gringo! I like that new 'Tormenta' song you dropped last month. So glad you stopped singing entirely about women's butts."

He didn't blush, per se, but she could see she'd touched on something delicate, so she turned her attention to Javier, hugging him, too. This time when the length of their bodies pressed together, her skin sparked across the surface and the air became thin, as if they were suddenly up very high. She pulled away and tried to shake it off so she could concentrate.

"I think they found another body. My uncle left in the middle of the night."

Javier stuffed his hands in his pockets. "Yeah, we just came from seeing him."

"What?" It wasn't that she was jealous, she was glad her uncle had bonded with her friends, but she had a serious case of FOMO—particularly when it came to zombie sightings, murders, and other supernatural occurrences.

"Yeah, they did find another body."

"Ghost sightings?"

Javier nodded. "Yeah. But he agrees with you and doesn't think it is the ghosts who are committing the murders."

Carlos nodded at her. "You saw 'em, too, Lupe?"

"Yep."

"Do you ever have a dull summer?" That famous grin spread across his perfect lips.

"No, but I'd sure like to try one!"

Javier was rocking back and forth on his heels. "Lupe, I overheard two cops talking. . . ."

The swaying was starting to make her nervous. Something was up.

"They were saying that if your uncle doesn't solve this case, and soon, the governor and the police commissioner are going to fire him."

If he had punched her in the gut she couldn't have been as thrown.

"What?"

No.

Her uncle was her foundation, the only truly solid thing in her life, and policing was that for him. His entire identity was tied to his job. . . . She wanted to sit down on the sidewalk. Then she wanted to punch someone. The emotions came one after another, like trains. "What, all the work he's done till now doesn't mean anything? After all he went through helping people during the hurricane?"

Carlos put up his hands. "Hey, we're on your side, hermana!"

"I know, I know." Now she was pacing like a tiger in a cage. "They can't do this! They just can't."

"Agreed. What should we do?" Just Javier's use of the word "we" was enough to calm her. This "friends who have each other's back" thing was new to her, so she was constantly amazed.

"Marisol and I went to see Professor Quiñones yesterday."

Carlos and Javier comically gaped at each other at the mention of the cranky old scholar's name, then broke into tear-producing laughter.

She tried not to join in, but it was hard. "Okay, okay, but the old coot was actually pretty helpful."

"At what? Cranky Old Bastard 101?"

"Or wait! How about Mocking the Gringa, graduate level?" They gave each other high fives, and Lupe lost patience.

"All right, all right, enough, you two! He actually told us that these ghostly appearances aren't new. They happened in the late 1920s also."

Carlos's bodyguard/driver guy stepped out of the SUV and called over to them. Why didn't that man have a neck? He nodded at Lupe with his unchanging serious expression. "Jefe, you have rehearsal at the resort in ten minutes."

Carlos looked at his phone. "Right. I gotta go. You two wanna come with? I'll drop you off at work, Javi."

Lupe grabbed her backpack and put it on the hood of Carlos's expensive car. Wait, why was it wet? Had she put it in a puddle? She unzipped the main compartment. "I might have to stop at our condo before we go, I'm not sure I have—" Her words backed up in her throat, and whatever she was about to say no longer mattered.

She was aware of the guys continuing their conversation, and then stopping as they noticed that she was just standing there. A rushing sound entered her ears and took away all other sound, her stomach lurching up, up, until she had to lean over and vomit in the gutter. A black, white, and red pattern was spinning before her eyes as she put her hands on her knees and swayed.

The first thing she became aware of was Javier's face in hers, his mouth opening and closing. His words started to come into focus.

"Lupe! What happened? Are you okay?"

His eyes were worried, so she nodded automatically though, really, she knew for a fact she wasn't okay at all.

Then Carlos's voice, pulled thin and tight. "Javier. You better come over here."

Then she remembered, and she gagged and vomited again.

Javier's voice then. "Jesucristo." She imagined he was making the sign of the cross.

She stood slowly, the street spinning a bit, until she could stand upright without feeling as if she would fall over. Then she looked over at the guys as they and the driver stared into the backpack, their faces pale.

"Lupe, how did a human heart get into your backpack?"

Chapter Eighteen

Javier

💀

"LUPE! SLOW DOWN!"

Javier and Carlos had to practically run to keep up with Lupe. They'd been trying to talk to her, but once she'd recovered from the shock, she'd demanded Carlos's jacket, wrapped up the blood-soaked backpack, and started walking very fast toward the condo.

Carlos pleaded, "Can we just stop and talk for a minute, hermana? This shit is real!"

The Escalade was driving slowly, keeping pace with them from the street, the driver watching the proceedings through the dark lenses of his sunglasses. The dude had to be horrified, too. It's not every day that someone finds a human heart in their backpack. But it had to look almost comical from a distance. An "unaware of the body part being carried down the street" distance.

Javier jogged up so that he was next to her, and Carlos followed suit on the other side.

"Lupe, we have got to call your uncle; you shouldn't be carrying it around. Isn't it evidence or something?"

"Yeah, and why can't we just put it in the back of my car?" Carlos offered for the tenth time.

Lupe glared at him. "I am not gonna be responsible for getting the blood of a murder victim in the back of your car, Papi Gringo. Can you imagine the press?"

"So, you use my two-thousand-dollar Armani jacket instead."

She shrugged. "It had to be leather. Otherwise it would have soaked right through."

"I'll never get that stain out," Carlos whined, as if this were about a piece of clothing.

"Oh, we're going to have to burn it."

Carlos gaped at her.

"Would you rather forever be associated with this?" She held up the leather-jacket-encased backpack.

"I see your point."

Javier was losing his patience with the two of them. "Look, I really have to insist we talk to Chief Dávila." He was barely able to talk, he was so winded. How much farther was the damn condo, anyway?

"Once again, he'll know about it." She didn't even seem out of breath. "I'm going to leave this outside our condo, let someone find it and report it, and he'll know."

"Can we just address the real issue? Someone broke into the condo and put this in *your* backpack. Not your uncle's, yours."

"Yes, I know that, Javier."

"But what we don't know is who the hell would have done this? It damn sure wasn't ghosts!"

"Why?" she asked over her shoulder.

His blood pressure was rising, he was certain. "Why what?"

"Why couldn't it be ghosts?"

"Well, first of all, as your uncle pointed out, they don't leave footprints."

"True. I'm still not ruling anything out."

Javier was exasperated. Wasn't she the one who had ruled them out two days ago? "The point is, you don't know who did this! And it's the danger to you that I'm concerned about." Javier realized he was beginning to sound like a grown-up. He didn't want to sound like a grown-up, but someone had to talk some sense.

She stopped.

"Thank God," Carlos wheezed, holding his hand to his chest.

Javier was grateful to have a moment to catch his breath, too.

"Maybe I was too quick to dismiss the captain based on the Facebook post."

Javier and Carlos stared at her.

Carlos sputtered. "Facebook post? What Facebook post?"

Javier added another question to the pile. "Captain who? Torres?"

She waved her hand at them. "Oh, it doesn't matter." And then she was off again, walking even faster than before.

"So, the top cop on the island could have put a human heart in your bag and 'it doesn't matter'?" Javier asked as they rushed to keep up.

"No, it matters. I mean, I can figure out who did it later, in the meantime I need to get rid of this . . . thing."

"Lupe!" Javier yelled, loudly. An old couple taking an early-morning walk gave him a look from across the street. He smiled and waved in apology. Not a good idea to call attention to the group when one of them was carrying the internal organ of a murder victim. But she still didn't stop. "We need to tell your uncle."

"No shit! Lupe, you're not making sense," Carlos said in a pleading voice.

She slowed for a second, looked at them, and said, "Guys, I appreciate your concern, but if he finds out about this, he'll send me home! Besides, given what you just told me, he has more important things to worry about. I have to help him solve this case so he doesn't lose his job."

Argh! Javier was doing his best not to scream in frustration, but it was so hard. She was the most stubborn person he'd ever met. And the most fearless.

"Girl, I don't want you to go, and I'm totally with you on helping your uncle, but I ain't gonna lie, that is the creepiest-ass shit I've ever seen, and I've seen some creepy-ass shit." Carlos had such a way with words when he was talking street.

Behind them Theo, the driver, echoed, "Some serious creepy-ass shit."

Lupe looked at the parcel. "Yes, it is. But I'm staying." And then she was off again, but they had arrived at the street where her uncle's rented condo was. She looked around the entrance and found that between the front steps of their building and the next, there was some space where garbage cans stood in a neat row like squat soldiers. She used the jacket as a sling and dropped the backpack into the corner, shadowed by the railing of the building's entrance.

"Isn't your uncle going to wonder why it's in your backpack?"

She shrugged. "I'll just tell him I lost it. They just emptied the garbage, so the maintenance guy will be pulling them inside later today and should find it. Now, where to burn the jacket . . ."

Carlos groaned.

Chapter Nineteen

Lupe

THEIR ARRIVAL AT the resort was very different from the first time Lupe had visited. Well, beyond the fact that the first time she hadn't just found a human heart in her backpack. But she was shocked by how much had been finished on the grounds in just a few days. When they dropped Javier off to start his workday, she saw that the fountain was spouting sparkling crystal-clear water into the morning air, there were trees and grass and flowers where there had just been sad dirt, and there were uniformed staff bustling in and out of the front door. But it was the reception that was markedly different. They were guided to a different building, the spa and entertainment center, on the other side of the property (the part that Lupe now knew was supposed to be protected under the nature reserve classification), and the SUV had barely rolled to a stop when they were surrounded by a crowd of people, all eagerly smiling at the vehicle.

"Wait, I didn't think there were this many press people on the entire island!"

Carlos smiled. "Oh, the owners have made sure to invite *all* the press for this event. From everywhere."

He stepped out, then offered her his hand in a showy way to help Lupe out of the car. Normally she rejected this kind of patriarchal gesture, but truthfully, she was a bit overwhelmed by the press of people all wanting something, and holding her friend's hand was a comfort.

Carlos stood close by her and whispered, "It's all right, amiga. They don't bite. Usually."

"Carlos, I'm a misanthrope from a town of, like, twenty people. This is *way* too much for me."

Among the calls and the assistant pleading for him to follow her, Lupe could hear the snap of photos.

"Papi Gringo! Papi Gringo! Is this your new girlfriend?"

Lupe sputtered, and Carlos put his arm around her. "No, no. This lovely is a dear friend of mine, Lupe Dávila from Vermont."

She could hear her name echo like it had been yelled in a canyon. "Vermont, is that in Canada?" She could sense frantic googling. Boy, were they going to be disappointed in her backstory.

Then someone hit internet-searching pay dirt. "Wait! Papi, you're dating the police chief's daughter?"

That one got Carlos sputtering. Talk about a reputation killer for a musical "bad boy."

Lupe called out "Niece! I'm Esteban Dávila's niece!" Not correcting anything else, kind of intentionally. Giving Carlos a hard time was a favorite hobby of hers.

Carlos was squirming now. She could get to like seeing him that way. It made him so much more . . . human.

"As I said, Lupe is just a friend."

She looked over at him. "Just?"

He smiled, beads of sweat rising on his forehead. "A very important friend."

Lupe watched one of the reporters turn to the other and air quote "important friend." This was too funny. But when she looked over at Carlos, she could see he was very uncomfortable, and she felt bad. He'd always been so good to her.

"Lupe!"

She spun around, only to see Sam's blond head bobbing through the press of people, a backstage pass hanging around his neck. She couldn't help but smile—the boy was so cute and so damn bouncy.

"Hey, Sam!" She gave him a big hug, then turned around to introduce him to Carlos. "Carlos, I'd like you to meet—"

Carlos held out his hand with a tight smile. "Hey, Sam. How's it going?"

They pumped each other's hands in that "mine is bigger than yours" way that men had and stared at each other tensely. "You know each other?"

Carlos shuffled a bit. "Yeah, Sam's dad's company sponsored my last concert."

"I think it was your best so far," Sam offered.

And they stood there.

"Okay . . ." Lupe was entertained. What was it about this Sam guy that brought out all this competitive weirdness in the men around her?

"I gotta go do a sound check before rehearsal." Carlos pointed to the stage, where technicians and staff crawled all over scaffolding like worker ants. "Lupe, you can hang out in the audience, if you like. Might be boring for a while though. Lots of 'check one, check two.'"

"I'd be happy to give you a tour of the property, Lupe. A lot's been done since you were last here," Sam offered.

"Yeah, I noticed that." But she still couldn't take her eyes off the two. So interesting. "I'd like that."

Sam took her arm, and he and Carlos grimly nodded at each other before they walked in different directions.

They weaved in and out of the crowd of staff, onlookers, and random people like a video game. The colors and faces and press of bodies made Lupe's head feel light. And this wasn't even the actual concert. What was it going to be like when there were a couple of thousand people pressed into the space? When they finally broke out of the crowd and arrived at the side of the main building, Lupe stopped and leaned on the wall.

"Damn, I have to catch my breath after that."

"Weird, huh? That guy draws a lot of people."

"Yeah, what's it going to be like tomorrow night? Totally out of control?"

Sam looked back over the heads of the crowd. "I don't even want to know."

She watched him as she straightened back up. "What's up between you two?"

His head snapped back. "What are you talking about?"

"Some weird tension."

Sam shrugged. "We're just from totally different lifestyles, I guess."

"Yeah. Tense between you and Javier, too."

Sam smiled. "*That's* because of you."

Lupe could feel the blood rushing to her face and took that opportunity to turn around toward the beach and let the breeze cool the blush. That's when she saw Javier standing at the edge of the patio, staring at them. She smiled and waved, but he just turned around and disappeared behind the building. Her waving hand dropped like a popped party balloon, and she felt a spark of anger light in her chest.

"Ready for the tour?" Sam held out his arm for her to take again, and she hooked hers in his gladly. She was not going to play Javier's petty game.

So why did she feel sick to her stomach?

They walked around the grounds, admiring all that had been done, talking about where tomorrow's events would take place, ending at a bandstand set up adjacent to the concert facilities. They climbed the metal scaffolding stairs and sat halfway up, admiring the view, listening to the "check, check" amplified from Carlos's concert stage area. She tried to enjoy the moment of relaxation, but the news Javier had shared that morning was haunting her, even more than the heart incident.

"Sam, I think my uncle might be in trouble."

"What? How?"

"Javier overheard some cops talking about how if he doesn't solve these crimes, the governor and the police commissioner were going to fire him."

He sighed. "I was afraid something like that might happen."

"What? Why?"

"My father has a lot of money invested in this venture, and he will do whatever it takes to protect it. And he has a lot of political pull."

"How much pull?"

"Like, all the way to the top."

"Not our paper towel–throwing president?"

Sam nodded. "They play golf together. He's a member at Mar-a-Lago."

Lupe's head started to throb. This was *so* much worse than she thought.

"You okay?"

She hadn't realized how long she'd been silent until she saw Sam's concerned face. "Oh, yeah. It's just . . ." She turned around to face him. "You know that point in *The Walking Dead* when you stop worrying about the zombies and realize the living people are actually the biggest threat?"

"Not my favorite show, but I think so."

"Kind of feels like that's where we're at now. The ghosts are the least of our problems." It was then that she realized something without a doubt: a serial killer had left the heart in her bag.

A *human* serial killer.

Chapter Twenty

Javier

JAVIER HAD WATCHED Sam and Lupe walking around the property from the vantage point of his work area. He guessed that the prince was showing the fair maiden the breadth of his holdings.

Everything the light touches is my kingdom.

Javier snorted, then looked around to make sure no one saw him cackling to himself. His coworkers already thought he was a weird, angry loner.

Actually, they're probably right.

But Sam really bugged him. That level of wealth was just not necessary. At one point he watched Lupe throw back her head of honey hair and laugh, like she was in some kind of shampoo commercial.

The whole thing was nauseating.

It was a good thing his job that day was whacking the soil with a garden spade, breaking it up and loosening it so it was ready for sod placement. He was able to spear his anger right into the ground and imagine it dissipating like ripples in a pond. The owners would get their perfect grass so they could act as if the hurricane never happened—wouldn't want the guests to see anything unfortunate!—and he could take his frustration out on the ground. Of course, that made no sense either: this poor island had been through enough.

He got lost in the work and the day sped by. There was something so satisfying about working the soil—*like going back to our beginnings.* He loved having the sound of the surf as a constant accompaniment, the midday sun warming his skin. It was as the sun was beginning to sink toward the horizon that he was picking up his tools and materials to stop for the day. He had an armful of implements when he noticed movement over in the trees next to the opening to the private beach.

Who was over there?

The rest of his coworkers had already knocked off for the day. He had only stayed late in the hopes of avoiding Lupe and Sam.

He tried to ignore it, but then he heard a shushing sound, like something being dragged over sand.

Was it the ghosts again? He looked around. No, he didn't think it was dark enough for that. But wait, why would it need to be dark for them to appear? Was that just in the movies?

Javier gently placed his stuff on the ground and contemplated running. He remembered the torn and skeletal faces of the ghosts, the moaning that formed ice in the pit of his stomach.

He looked around again, frantic.

No one.

Not a soul.

He really was out there alone. He thought of the dark, wet heart in Lupe's bag.

No one would even hear him scream.

Scraping sounds, the rustle of dried fronds on the ground.

Javier's heart pounded in his chest. His mouth was dry.

"C'mon, man. Calm down." His voice sounded thin, unconvincing, but he made the decision to go check out the noise, wondering in that exact moment if it was a really stupid idea. It always was in the movies, wasn't it? But he was no coward. He bent down and quietly picked up his hand tiller from the pile of gardening implements. The long-handled tool with its sharp spikes at the end was an ideal weapon. Wouldn't help much with ghosts, but he felt better with it in his hands.

He crouched and tiptoed over toward the beach, staying close along the strip of bushes and small, young palm trees they'd planted the week before. What was he doing? He was no cop. Christ, he could barely take care of himself! But he forced himself to keep going, his fingers white from his tight grip on the wooden handle of the tiller. He almost laughed out loud. He must look ridiculous! But his sense of self-preservation kept him quiet.

Just before he reached the opening to the beach, a shadow lengthened in front of him, and he jolted backward. He hadn't been imagining things! There was someone there. But who? Reflexively he put his hand over his heart, wanting it to stay in his chest.

Voices, tinny voices.

It was the blurt of a police radio.

What?

A huge flood of relief washed over him.

It wasn't anything supernatural. It was someone who worked with the police. But in his life that wasn't exactly a comfort either: until Esteban Dávila the police hadn't given him a warm and fuzzy feeling of protecting and serving. Then he remembered what Lupe had said about a possible serial killer, and something about Torres. He would have to check it out anyway, but at least he had a chance against a human.

After last year's rumble with El Cuco he wanted nothing to do with the supernatural.

He pushed a few branches aside so he could see who was rustling near the sand.

He saw the top of a bald head shining in the setting sun, ringed with short, white hair, sweat snaking down the pale brown flesh of the man's skull. Whoever it was wiped his face and head with a cloth handkerchief, hands shaking. When he put a hat on and turned around, Javier recognized Captain Torres's reddening face. What was he doing over here looking so nervous? Had Lupe been right? Was he a . . . serial killer?

Javier ducked a bit to make sure the older policeman wouldn't see him. Torres was pulling a small motorboat farther from the water and into the bushes, talking to himself in a string of muttered words. Then he looked around, finding the coast seemingly clear, and started back toward the opening in the trees, out of breath from just walking across the sand in his shiny police dress shoes. How could a person who was that out of shape manage to be a police captain? And how would he have the energy to cut a heart out of someone, let alone five someones?

Still, Javier knew from personal experience when a man was up to no good.

Chapter Twenty-one

Lupe

💀

DRIVING BACK TO the condo that evening, Lupe and her uncle both seemed to be lost in their own thoughts. She'd spent the day with Sam, eating lunch at the spa, driving around the property in a golf cart, even playing a quick game of tennis on the brand-new courts (badly, though he was patient with her; tennis was not her game). It truly felt like she was playing a role after the events of the morning, but she needed to be occupied when someone found the backpack.

At two o'clock the call from her uncle had come. They had found something at their condo, and did she know where her backpack was? She told him she'd lost it and he seemed to accept that. But he was moving them elsewhere, and he wouldn't pick her up until later that afternoon.

Sam had been a very gracious host, and she tried her best to relax, but, truth be told, even Sam seemed distracted. For Lupe, it was finding out about the threat to her uncle's job that ensured she thought about little else.

Her uncle's phone rang. No, it really *rang*. He'd programmed his flip phone with that old-fashioned phone ring that sounded like a dentist drill and a shrieking banshee had a baby.

"Dávila. Yeah . . . a boat? No. Call if you see anything else. Bueno." *Click.*

Her tío's conversations were like shorthand, or something. "What's up?"

"That was Utierre."

Her throat tightened. Why was Javier calling her uncle? Did he tell him about the heart? No, he was too calm for it to have been about that. But then what? She had to play this carefully. She worked at making her voice sound casual. "Oh yeah? What did Javier want?"

Her uncle looked over at her through narrowed eyes, like he totally saw through her faux-casual ruse. "He saw Torres dragging a motorboat into the bushes at the resort."

"Hernán?"

Her uncle shook his head. "No, his father. Javier said he looked like he was up to something, but I told him I didn't think that's anything to worry about. The man is a clown, but he's not dangerous."

Lupe said nothing. Their little encounter during the ride from the ferry hadn't felt exactly safe. But now wasn't the time to have *that* discussion. Sitting next to him, all she could think about was the threat to his job. She knew Esteban hated prying—he was a private-type creature like her father—but there were questions eating at her from inside like termites. She had to ask, but she was unsure how to best approach it.

She coughed. "Tío. Do you ever get tired of your job?" Sure, it was roundabout, but she had a plan.

He looked over at her with his half smile in the darkening of the car. "Seguro, of course. I think everyone does sometimes. Why do you ask?"

She shrugged. "I don't know. I guess I wondered what you and Titi would do if you weren't a cop anymore."

He was silent for a few beats, then said, "I don't know, I suppose I've never considered the possibility. I've been sure of this path since before I was your age."

Okay, the conversation was only making her feel worse, but she had to go on. "But what would you do? For work, I mean. Would you retire?"

A scoff, like she'd proposed he put lobsters in his ears. "Sobrina, as your grandfather Carl always said, 'you stop working and you die.'"

"Um, but isn't he . . . like . . . dead?"

"Exactly my point!" He smiled. Then he sighed. "Well, your aunt has always been after me to move to Miami and work with her brother." A laugh, then he shifted his focus to a snarl in traffic due to loose chickens running to and fro in the road.

She looked out at the chickens, running with their ridiculous gait. "Looks like Vermont. But we have to wait for cows to cross the road."

"Well, that happens here, too, but less frequently, I would imagine. Chickens, however, are everywhere. And these do not appear in any hurry to 'cross the road.'" He laughed his deep, rolling belly laugh that she loved so much.

But Lupe just stared out the window. She didn't feel like laughing, even at the hens running back and forth in a flurry of feathers. Coming down to this place every year, staying with her aunt and uncle, was what got her through the school year. It just wouldn't be the same in Florida. Florida? Ugh.

They finally were able to move, and slowly rolled into Esperanza, to the little hotel her uncle had moved them to. She looked at the storefronts shuttered for the night, the men playing dominoes on folded tables outside the open-air bar, their laughter ringing out into the night. She smiled at the old couple rocking in their chairs on the front porch of a little house, the conversation as leisurely as the evening heat, and at a passing car blaring the latest reggaeton hit into the air, the windows thumping with the bass line. The waves kissing the shore beyond the malecón. There was something about this place that spoke to a part of her that hadn't awoken before last summer, something she didn't want to lose.

She had just climbed into bed with the latest thick Chuck Wendig fungal pandemic novel when her phone buzzed. Marisol. When she answered she could hear the line was clear and crackle-free.

"Hey! You have good cell service! You must be in San Juan."

"Yes, I'm back in civilization. For the night, anyway. I was doing some research into the situation out there."

Marisol wasn't a small-talk type. It made Lupe smile.

"Something Quiñones said has been bothering me," she continued.

"Everything that man says bothers me. What in particular?" Yeah, no way she was going to tell her about the backpack on the phone. She'd wait until they saw each other in person. Maybe she'd wait even longer.

"What he said about the land not being blocked off for natural conservation. I did some digging and came across some things that don't make sense. There's this retired naval officer, a Lieutenant Colonel Kevin Jones, I think we should talk to. He still lives on the island, never left. Something weird went down and I think he knows what it is."

"Yeah, the navy pulled out."

"Right, but why?"

Lupe reviewed what she knew. "The protests?"

"No, I think something else happened, and this Jones guy might know about it."

Something to do! Thank goodness. If there was one thing Lupe detested it was inactivity. "Great! When you comin'?"

"I think I'll take the eight a.m. ferry in the morning. It's going to be a zoo, thanks to the resort opening, and they don't let nonresidents bring cars on a *regular* day. Can you or your uncle pick me up at the boat dock?"

Chapter Twenty-two

Marisol

MARISOL HAD TO park far away from the ferry terminal in Ceiba. The public lot was full to overflowing with cars and it was only 7:30 a.m. She had to navigate through boxy news vans and hundreds of protestors, their signs, clean and smelling of recently applied paint, balanced on shoulders as they slowly made their way with the crowds merging onto the ferries. The worst were the giggling teenage Papi Gringo fans, T-shirts featuring Carlos's face tight across their breasts, their eyes hidden behind overpriced Papi Gringo brand sunglasses.

Damn.

Didn't they know the island was in turmoil?

Actually, Marisol was torn between being pleased to see them acting like normal teenagers and returning to normal life after the nightmare that Maria brought, and newly disappointed that they hadn't all become activists fighting for what was right.

Okay, so she knew that was far-fetched, but a girl could dream.

Three ferries came and went, people stuffed in like sardines, before Marisol finally was able to get on a boat. After Maria they didn't even have all the regular ferries back in service, but the developers had brought in private ferries from Florida, so they had extra ones running for the grand opening. Too bad they couldn't use those resources to help Puerto Rico when there wasn't money to be made. Sigh. But between the people on the line and the people on the ferry, she had filled almost all the pages of her petition. She hated approaching strangers, but her counselor said human contact was good for her. She preferred dogs.

There wasn't anyone who looked like a VIP among the other ferry riders. No surprise there. They were probably on the small private planes and buzzing helicopters that would start coming to and from the island like bees to a hive in the midafternoon. The rich, famous, and political had to sleep off their hangovers first.

She was wondering how she would find Lupe in the bedlam of disembarking when she saw her pony-tailed head near a police cruiser with its blue lights blazing. Marisol smirked. She could never lose Lupe in a crowd. As she walked over, she saw her friend talking to a short but handsome officer, his face lit up in the way that men and boys tended to do when they talked to Lupe. As far as Marisol could tell, they never hit on her openly—Lupe was not exactly approachable in her snowy Vermont winter kind of way—but when she was nice to them it was like the sun was shining on them alone.

But a cop? Not exactly her type. Lupe tended toward the bad-boy variety. She was going to have to get the scoop on this situation.

Lupe saw Marisol and literally skipped up to her, messy ponytail bouncing. She threw herself at Marisol and hugged her hard. Oh great: another hug. As if they hadn't seen each other in months instead of just two days ago.

"Okay, that's enough hugging. Hell, you've used up your

quota already and it's been less than forty-eight hours!" Marisol pulled back with a smirk, but when they separated, she could tell something was wrong. When Lupe was worried her forehead did this crinkly thing, right between her eyebrows. Marisol looked over at the way-too-cheery cop standing next to them. She'd have to ask her later when they didn't have surveillance.

He greeted her in fluent and respectful Spanish. "Marisol, this is Hernán—I mean, Officer Torres."

Hernán, huh? He looked like a gringo but spoke Spanish without an accent. Yeah, she would have to get the scoop. *And* she would have to stalk him on social media just to be sure.

Then Torres put out his hand and she shook it, watching the surprise in his eyes at the firmness of her grip. Her brother, Vico, had taught her how to shake hands when she was little. He used to say, "You gotta know how to navigate the world, Mari. Don't take shit from anyone, you hear me? I won't be around forever to defend your ass." Of course, he was the one who gave her the most shit, and then he starting dealing drugs and got himself killed by the boogeyman.

Won't be around forever.

No shit, hermano.

Torres retrieved his hand with an awkward head bob, then turned to Lupe. "You sure you don't want me to drive you two wherever you're going?" He gestured around to the mass of people flowing past them, then put his hands on his gun belt in stereotypical cop fashion.

Lupe smiled, but it didn't go to her eyes. It was her wary smile. "No, thanks. We're just going to do some sightseeing."

Sightseeing? Lupe never did sightseeing. They weren't sightseeing types.

"But I grew up here. If you want to tell me where you're going, I can act as a tour guide."

"Really, we'll be fine. Thank you." The "thank you" smacked of finality, conversation over, y punto.

Ooh, the Vermont winter winds were blowing.

He nodded—there was no arguing with Lupe when she put her foot down—but even so, he seemed reluctant to take his gaze off her. He gave in and opened the door of the cruiser. "I'll at least get you out of here."

"Great!" Lupe walked over to a large golf cart that was tucked behind the cruiser. She smiled at Marisol, this time with her eyes. "This is our ride."

Marisol smiled back. "Now *this* looks like fun." She climbed into the passenger seat, throwing her backpack in the space behind the seats, and held on to the metal frame that held the windshield as Lupe did a U-turn. It turned out to be good that Torres was in front of them, as the flashing lights and occasional blaring of the siren cut a path through the crowds. Once they were free of the ferry traffic, Lupe waved at Torres, who turned left as they turned right.

Lupe had taped a paper with printed directions to the cart's dashboard. GPS had been iffy on Vieques *before* the hurricane. Now? Who knew. Once they were bouncing down the roads, wind blowing their hair behind them in the open-air vehicle, Marisol turned her body around to face Lupe. "So, Hernán, huh?"

"Yeah, Hernán." But her smile turned down, just a bit.

"What's the story there?"

Lupe shrugged. "He's fine."

"Fine, huh?"

"Yeah."

But Marisol wasn't going to let it stand at that. She just stared at her.

Lupe threw up her hands. "Okay, fine. His father is the police captain on the island and given how threatening the old man was to me, it's useful to have his son on my side."

"His police captain father threatened you? Does he *know* who your uncle is?"

"Yep. He told me if I told Tío he would deny it."

"Well, clearly the man has no idea who you are either. You *are* going to tell your uncle, right?"

Lupe sighed. "Tío has enough to worry about right now."

Marisol just kept staring.

"I'll explain later, I promise. Besides, I'm not entirely sure that Torres senior isn't the one cutting out peoples' hearts."

"What? You think the highest-ranking cop on the island is a serial killer?"

"I didn't say that, I just said I'm not sure he's *not.* In order to eliminate him, I figure being friendly with the son will help get me more information on the father."

Marisol whistled between her teeth. "Ooh! Cold, girl. Even for you. The guy is sweet on you."

Lupe did that one-sided smile. "'Sweet on me?' Where did you get that expression? 1956?"

"You know what I mean."

She shrugged again, her hair gradually escaping from her loose ponytail and blowing back as if relieved to be set free. "He offered to escort me to the rental place to get the cart and then to the ferry to navigate the cars. It helped." She turned down a rut-etched dirt road, the sun peeking from behind the dark clouds and filtering through the canopy of leaves in strips. It was still beautiful despite the storm damage.

"I'm amazed there were carts to rent with all the goings-on."

"Oh, there weren't."

Then they said at the same time, "Tío Esteban." They laughed. Lupe's big, gruff uncle had become an uncle to Marisol, too. During the hurricane, when all her family had been overcrowded in the water-logged condo in Isla Verde, he'd shown up out of the blue with bottles of water, flashlights, cell phone chargers, food, and cash. Marisol's abuela cried when she opened the door and there he was, long arms loaded with treasure. Truth be told, Marisol cried, too, but she was careful not to let him see. Along with all he was doing to help everyone on the island, he still managed to check in on them every few days, bringing the building manager kerosene for the generator that was running the elevators and emergency lights to the twenty-story building, sending officers when he couldn't make it.

She told Lupe about his visits but couldn't convey just how much it meant to her and her family. They would never, ever, forget his kindness. Her abuela insists he's an angel, and Marisol teases her about it, but doesn't argue.

They pulled up to a faded, salmon-colored, one-story home tucked into a copse of stripped palms, their short, bright new fronds like paint on the end of a chewed-on brush. Marisol thought that the house had probably looked sad even before the hurricane.

She and Lupe jumped out of the golf cart and called through the gated front door.

"Hello?"

Sounds of birdsong and water flowing nearby. That was all.

"Hello!"

Nothing. Silence from the house, but not the empty kind. Marisol was sure he was there. She thought about her marine cousin and had an idea. "Lieutenant Colonel? We need your help!"

A beat of silence. Then clipped, clean footsteps from the back of the house. Then it hit her that, though this had been her idea, she knew nothing about this man. He could be insane. Christ, *he* could be the serial killer! Marisol pictured him coming to the front in full camo, a machine gun expertly held in his hands. Shit. "Is it getting really hot out here?" she asked Lupe, fanning her face like a crying beauty queen.

The man who came up to the gate was no Arnold Schwarzenegger, but he was pretty fit for an old guy in his Levi's jeans and lean-fitting T-shirt. He was short for a man, probably 5'7" or so, his salt-and-pepper hair kept navy cropped. He was probably handsome, in a George Clooney kind of way, but his eyes were tired. She could even say they were haunted.

"Can I help you girls?" he asked in a clipped Southern accent.

Girls.

Ugh.

But Lupe put on her best newscaster smile and launched right into it. "Lieutenant Colonel, we—"

"Don't call me that."

Lupe sputtered for a minute; her soliloquy interrupted. "Oh . . . okay." The last syllable of "okay" rose up in question. A pause, then she continued. "Mr. Jones, I—"

"Mr. Jones was my father," he said as he took keys from his pocket and unlocked the gate. "I'm Jones. Just Jones." He opened the door and gestured for them to come in.

"Okay, Just Jones . . ."

Marisol shot a look at Lupe. She really could push it. But then she noticed that Jones was smiling.

They introduced themselves as he led them into a surprisingly bright kitchen, clean and smelling of fresh bread and ammonia. Jones pointed to two metal chairs under a square metal table with a sparkly white-and-blue top.

"So, Jones . . ." Lupe grimaced a bit, as if the name didn't fit in her mouth right. It probably didn't: when you're raised by a Puerto Rican you have trouble calling adults anything other than señor, señora, or doña. "We are doing some research on the land that the new resort is being built on."

Marisol broke in. "Is it true that the navy stole the property out from under three thousand people and forcibly relocated them to St. Croix?"

Jones's eyes looked weary. "Yes, though they were compensated."

"How much?"

Jones practically mumbled, "I think it was something like fifty dollars an acre."

Lupe laughed. "Even back then I don't imagine that was much money."

"And it's not like they had a choice, right?" Marisol said.

Lupe straightened up, bringing the conversation back on track. "But we're really wondering about why the navy left the island."

"The true story, that is," Marisol added.

Jones smiled at her with a small glint in his eyes. "You get right to the point, young lady. I like that." He sat back in his chair. "Well, what have you heard?"

Lupe spoke next. "Only what's in the press. That they were forced out due to protests."

Jones shook his head. "That isn't why we left."

Marisol noted that he said "we" left, but in fact he was still here. Interesting.

He seemed lost in his own memories for a moment. When he began talking again, both girls started a bit. "We tried to stay. We designated the . . . problem area as a nature preserve. Forbade trespassing. But it didn't stop."

"The trespassing?"

He shook his head. "No, the . . . incidents."

Marisol knew that there was so much happening in the navy man's pauses; she even sensed something painful. Well, he liked straightforwardness. "What incidents?"

He jerked his head and looked at Marisol, looked at her as if he were just seeing her for the first time. "I served in the Gulf War. I was a cop in Miami for ten years." He stared into her eyes in a vacant-but-intense way. "And I was scared."

Shivers lifted the hair on Marisol's arms. She locked eyes with Lupe, then turned back to Jones. "Scared of what?"

He didn't answer. Lupe put her hand on top of his and he looked at her. Girl was so good at that nurturing type of thing. "Jones, scared of what?"

He let it out like a breath he'd been holding for years. "The ghosts! Glowing ghosts!"

At the outburst, Lupe jumped up and pulled her hand away in surprise.

His eyes flipped back and forth as if he were watching something cross in front of them. Marisol could see him work to calm down, to level his voice. "It was after we started building a munitions storage building. The night we broke ground, these lights came out of the trees when we worked late. It was like the glow of the bio bay, that blue light!"

Marisol noticed that he seemed to have forgotten they were even there. Good, he was more likely to say more that way. Lupe just looked pale; the man's story probably brought up memories of her own ghostly sighting.

"At first, we thought it was the guys playing a joke on us, you know? There were some pranksters in our unit. But then I looked closer and saw that they were . . . dead things. All rotted. And they made this noise, not a moan exactly, more a low hum." He gestured to his mouth. "I could feel it rattling my teeth, it was so strong. We tried to talk to our CO about it, but he thought we were—"

"Crazy," Marisol interjected.

He nodded. "Yes." Then he gathered both of Marisol's hands in his with a lurch, startling her a bit.

Lupe was the hand-holder; why was he taking hers? But

damned if she was going to pull them away and interrupt his train of thought.

"But we weren't crazy. We'd all seen them. We're not *all* crazy." He was almost pleading with Marisol, his eyes glassy.

She smiled a little, patted his hands awkwardly, and extricated hers. Sure, she felt for the guy, but he sure was acting odd.

"When command realized that we were all seeing things, they thought that there was some mind-altering poison in the soil, or the fruit, or the rum. It was starting to look bad for them, so they pulled out before the media got ahold of it."

"Did the ghosts ever . . . ?" Lupe seemed to be choosing her words carefully, something neither of them was particularly good at. ". . . kill anyone in your unit?"

"And cut out their hearts?" Marisol added.

Lupe gave her a look. "Thanks."

"You're welcome."

He looked from one to the other, seeming surprised. "No. Nothing like that. But they were angry. You could feel it. It was coming off them like heat." His eyes were doing that thing again. Marisol wondered if there was something really wrong with Jones.

"There's something I don't understand." Lupe crossed her arms as she thought. "Why didn't *you* leave, too, if you were so scared? Why do you still live here?"

He turned his body to face her, his eyes wide. "I couldn't leave! I can't leave! They won't let me leave!"

Lupe inspected him. "The navy?"

"No!" Then he looked around and whispered, "The ghosts!"

Silence for a beat.

Then Lupe said in a careful voice, "The ghosts tried to stop you?"

"No! I'm not even going to try! They won't let me leave; I just know it."

And there it was conclusively: the lights were on, but no one was home.

As Marisol glanced around the small house, or at least as far as she could see from her kitchen perch, she realized there was no sign of a spouse, or a roommate. Poor guy needed treatment, and here he was hiding out in the mountains, alone.

As if reading her mind, he said, "The locals, here on the island, they don't think I'm crazy. Most of them, or someone they know, have seen for themselves. *They* understand."

Lupe put her hand on his shoulder. "I've seen them. We don't think you're crazy either."

Marisol added, "Well, not for that anyway. The not-leaving-the-island thing . . . well . . ."

Lupe's voice was extra gentle, as if she were compensating for Marisol's lack of sensitivity. "Did you ever figure out what it was that they wanted? The . . . ghosts, I mean."

He shook his head, slowly and sadly. "If we had, maybe they wouldn't have come back."

They both looked at each other, then back at him. "Have you seen them lately?" Lupe asked.

He shook his head again. "No. But I've heard talk in town. And that sound started again, the humming. I can feel it at night. That's why I couldn't sleep these past few weeks."

It seemed he had good reasons for being . . . the way he was. Just like Marisol had the summer before, when she was part of the El Cuco curse. It made her . . . angry. Violent. With a sudden rush of empathy, Marisol wanted to make him feel better. To comfort him. "Jones." He looked at her. "We're going to figure out what they want. I promise you."

His eyes filled, and he nodded at Marisol.

As if by the same cue, they stood and started for the door,

leaving their host to wipe his eyes on his T-shirt before he let them out with a simple "Bye," locked the gate, and disappeared once more into his little house.

As they climbed into the bright green golf cart, Lupe stopped, then looked over with a half smile. "It's my job to make the promises we probably can't keep."

Marisol lifted her eyebrows. "Well? Aren't you always telling me to be more positive?"

Chapter Twenty-three

Javier

JAVIER HAD JUST hauled in the last of the ten-gallon tins of sealant that he had used on the stones of the patio to the basement, and was contemplating lying down right there on the grass, despite the parade of workers, guests, and random men in suits that hummed around him as if he weren't there. He frowned at the thought. Laborers were supposed to be invisible. Thoughts like this made his blood boil. Actually, these days most thoughts made his blood boil. He'd picked a hell of a decade to stop using drugs.

"Hey, don't they give you a lunch break around here?"

Javier looked up and saw Carlos rounding the corner, a shopping bag in each hand giving off a warm, buttery scent that made Javier's mouth water. He looked at his watch, blew the dust off it, and was surprised to find it was well past noon. He tipped his head toward the beach area silently. Carlos nodded back and they both headed to the break in the trees. They settled down behind the greenery so they couldn't be seen by Javier's foreman, and immediately tucked into the food. It was piping hot and tasted home cooked. The pork was moist and marinated, the taste of rosemary and red wine dancing on the back of his tongue. So much better than the soggy cheese sandwich that had been cooking forgotten in the truck all morning.

"Man, where did you get this? I haven't found food this good on the island. Did someone's abuela cook it?"

Carlos smiled his gato smile. "Well, if the abuela studied at Le Cordon Bleu in Paris."

Javier had no idea what the man was going on about, but the food was so good he didn't care.

Carlos continued, realizing that the reference meant nothing to Javier. "I flew my personal chef in from San Juan. She's an artist."

Javier licked the pork juices off his fingers and smiled. "Is she single?"

"She's fifty-six."

Javier shrugged. "Does she need an honorary nephew? I'm just saying."

They sat and just chewed for a while as the hubbub of sound continued over the trees and behind them and the surf teased the shore, back and forth. Belly full, Javier closed his eyes. He hadn't been this relaxed in days.

"So, Javier. I gotta talk to you about something."

The food stuck in Javier's throat. He knew it couldn't last, and he found his temper flaring. "Can't we just sit, quiet for a minute? Why does everything have to be so damn serious these days?"

Carlos dropped the pork rib he'd been holding and turned on Javier. "What the hell is wrong with you *these days*, Javi?"

"Man, what are you talking about?" Javier pretended that his heart wasn't pounding on the inside of his ribs, that it hadn't been like that for eight months. He never could hide much from his best friend.

"Lately, you don't answer your phone, you ignore my messages, you get pissed off at the rain that falls. Ever since—"

The pounding rushed up into Javier's face. "Since what? Since the island almost got wiped off the damn map? Since people have been suffering for months with no power and no running water and our 'government' has done shit about it? Since I had no choice but to work for the enemy?" His arms gestured wildly at the resort property all around them. "Doesn't any of this even bother you, Carlos?"

"Of course it does! What, do you think I'm heartless?" He seemed to catch himself on the last word and took a deep breath. "Look, first of all, you know any money you need is yours, right?"

"And you know I don't take handouts!"

"Fine, but I'm there for you if you need it. And second, I feel what's happened to our island. Here." He pounded his chest with his fist, like he did onstage, but with more feeling. "I've been working with charities left and right, trying to bring attention to our cause. Right after the hurricane I sent my plane back and forth from the States with supplies."

"Yeah, I saw that on the national news." It came out snarkier than he had intended. Javier looked at Carlos then, *really* looked. Then the question that had been scratching with sharp claws at the back of his mind for months came out. "Why aren't you outraged?" He waved his arms in frustration. "Why isn't everyone outraged?"

Carlos shrugged his shoulders. "What good would that do? Other than raising our blood pressure. Look, I didn't come here to talk about this, I—"

Javier threw his hands up. "Oh, right, you've been wanting to talk about you. Your favorite subject, huh, Papi Gringo?" The minute it came out of his mouth he wished he could yank it back in, settle it down into the dark cloud festering in his belly. Carlos didn't have a selfish bone in his body and Javier knew it.

"See? Right there!" Carlos pointed at him. "You didn't used to be such a dick!"

Their voices were raised, but underneath them Javier noticed a rhythmic thumping sound that was getting louder and louder. Carlos seemed to notice it, too, and stopped, just when something ran between them in a cloud of sand. Javier jumped. "What the hell is that?"

Then he saw a poofy little dog skidding to a stop just beyond them.

The dog had something in its mouth, but Javier was too busy lamenting the layer of sand on top of the lunch feast to investigate what. "Aw, dog! ¡Fuera! Get out of here! Shoo!"

But the dog noticed Carlos, dropped whatever he had been carrying, and leapt into his lap, jumping and licking his face.

Javier was surprised. Carlos had never liked dogs before. "Must be the pork juice on your face."

"Stop it, Gwendolyn!" Carlos rubbed her furry ears and cooed in her squished face. "Who's my good girl?"

Javier stared at the tough Papi Gringo, kissing the perfumed white shih tzu with the plaid Gucci bow in her hair. "Um, you two know each other?"

Carlos was giggling. For real. "Yeah, she's the owner's dog."

Just then they both heard calling coming toward them from behind the trees.

"Gwen! C'mere girl! Gwen?" Then Sam appeared on the beach and did a comical double take when he saw Javier and Carlos and their sand-covered picnic. At the sight of Sam, Gwendolyn took off toward him, then began circling his legs and barking in a high-pitched, nails-on-a-chalkboard voice.

Javier chuckled, a bit meanly if he was completely honest. "That your dog?"

Sam gave him a level look. The judgment was not lost on him. "No. She's my stepmother's." But he smiled at the ridiculous creature bouncing around anyway. "And she's a monster."

Javier watched Sam nod at Carlos, and Carlos nod back.

"You two know each other, too?"

"Yeah. Sam's dad sponsored this concert. He's sponsored a couple of them."

Gwen froze, sniffed the air, then ran back, seeming to remember whatever she had been carrying, and Sam yelled, "Drop it!" She obeyed, but then ran around Javier, barking. Oh. Fun. He just loved irritating little designer dogs.

"Um, guys? I think we have a problem." Javier had heard that voice from Carlos before. It was never good.

Sam and Javier walked over to where Carlos was crouched in the sand, a long, bleached white bone lying in front of him.

"That's a femur. A human femur." Sam's voice was tight and incredulous.

Hell, they all were incredulous. "How do you know that, man?" Javier was hoping he was wrong.

Sam's gaze skittered around a bit, as if he were embarrassed. "I'm in pre–veterinary med at Cornell."

Javier rolled his eyes. "Of course you are."

"Can we focus?" Carlos's voice was short, impatient. "There's a piece of a dead human here." Carlos picked it up and examined it. Then he looked over at the dog. "Where did she get this?" Noticing that he had her bone, Gwen grabbed an end in her mouth and pulled, growling and snorting, as if she were an actual dog or something. When Carlos wouldn't drop it, she gave up and took off in the direction she'd originally come from, barking as she ran.

Javier jumped up. "We should follow her! She might be going to get another one."

But Sam was already running after her, yelling "Gwen! Come back here!"

Carlos and Javier broke into a run, all three of them dodging between trees, jumping over vines, following the sound of Gwen's barking. They reached the long trail of large marble paving stones that the dog seemed to be following.

They came to a stop where the path ended, right in front of the landscaper's storage building, a large but simple concrete box with a padlocked door.

Javier couldn't help but think of kissing Lupe right there. Heat rose behind his face.

"What the hell is this building?" Sam asked.

"Landscaper storage," Javier answered. "The resort owners wanted the equipment stored away from the guests. Guess the sight of a weed wacker ruins rich people's vacations." He glared at Sam. "So, they tore down a partial structure that was started here and never finished, dug in a larger foundation, and built this monstrosity."

The barking started again, the sound coming from behind the squat building. The three guys ran around the building and found a huge pile of dirt and rocks against the trees. The barking had stopped, and the dog was nowhere in sight.

Sam was about to say something when Gwen came running from around the back of the pile with what looked like a finger bone in her mouth, her tail wagging like a hairy white flag. Javier watched her take off back toward the resort. He was about to ask why Sam wasn't going after her when he realized he was alone.

He walked around the back of the pile and found Carlos and Sam staring openmouthed. As he came closer, Javier saw among the slabs of rich, brown bulldozed earth hundreds of bleached white bones.

"Jesucristo," Carlos said under his breath as he made the sign of the cross.

Javier crouched down and looked at what the dirt revealed. "Wow. There are so many." He took a stick and lifted a shredded, half-eaten piece of rough fabric—burlap, or cotton.

"Think that's a shroud?" Sam asked.

"That's what I would guess."

"What happened here?" Sam wondered rhetorically, his voice quiet and reverent as if they were in a church. Perhaps they were.

But none of them had answers, and given the apparent age of the findings, Javier doubted they'd find any on their own.

Carlos's phone jangled with the first notes of last year's breakout hit, and he answered it as he walked around the pile and out of sight.

Javier realized that he and Sam were alone, kind of, and the silence became awkward. He stood up and brushed off his jeans, though he doubted any dirt had gotten on them. Still, his skin felt like it was crawling, and he was fighting off the urge to run all the way to the terminal, take the next ferry off this island, and never return.

But that wasn't an option. Was running ever really an option for him?

"So . . ." Sam said.

"So?" Javier asked, harsher than he had intended. What could he possibly have to talk about with this rich gringo? He'd probably never cleaned a toilet in his life. Javier didn't have any respect for someone who'd never had to clean a toilet. Besides, he was hanging around with Lupe. Javier didn't like that but knew he couldn't say anything. Lupe would dump his ass faster than a Vermont summer. Luckily Carlos's voice broke the awkward silence.

"Um, guys? I think I found something," he called from the front of the storage building.

Javier and Sam practically jumped in their enthusiasm to escape and arrived together to find Carlos crouched down next to one of the paving stones.

"I thought the shape of these was odd." Carlos dug two fingers underneath the edge of the third stone from the building and lifted it up. "Shit. I thought so." Then he flipped it over, the large marble slab hitting the packed dirt with a deep *thump*, and as he brushed off the layer of dirt, Javier realized what they were seeing. Then he looked at the line of similar stones that led all the way to the resort grounds.

He swallowed. "They're tombstones?"

"They can't all be . . . Can they?" Sam's voice was tight, and he ran over to a stone a few yards away, put his fingers under the edge, and peeked beneath. "God. I think they are."

Javier crouched down and did the same to the first one, closest to the building's gated doorway. "'Antonia Vargas,'" he read. 'Born February 17, 1920, died September 13, 1928.' Damn, she was only eight years old."

"This one was forty-three, Ofelia Gutiérrez. She died on the same day, September 13, 1928," Sam responded.

"This one, too. Same death date." Javier brushed the rest of the dirt off the carvings. His phone rang and all three of them jumped. Cue nervous laughter, hands over hearts. He looked at the screen. Lupe. "Hello?"

"Javier, Marisol and I just talked to this retired military guy, and he said the navy left because of the ghosts." She always did get right to the point.

"Yeah, I'm afraid we made quite a discovery here."

"What? You did? Wait, who's 'we'? Where's 'here'?"

"Me, Carlos, and Sam. And we're behind the main resort building."

He could hear her breathing and an up and down jostling of the phone. "Marisol and I just got to the resort. We had to walk the last mile and a half. Too many damn people trying to get in."

"Well, we'll meet you out back. We . . . have to talk." That was an understatement. "Then find your uncle."

"We're here."

Her words echoed. They were close. He clicked End. "Lupe! ¡Ven acá! Over here!"

Chapter Twenty-four

Marisol

MARISOL WAS FOLLOWING Lupe into the trees and bushes that fed into the formerly "protected" part of the nature preserve. She was fascinated with the marble pathway. Who puts marble paving stones leading into a forest? She stepped from one to the next like a game of hopscotch until she crashed right into Lupe. She laughed and grabbed her friend by the shoulders to catch her balance but realized everyone was silent. And just standing there.

The three guys were spread along the end of the path, each standing over a pulled-up stone. Lupe was staring down at the closest one, the one nearest the boy she assumed was Sam. That was when Marisol took a good look at the stone.

"Dios mio." She automatically made the sign of the cross. Then she looked back the way they had come, back to the resort. "But . . . there are dozens of them."

Javier pointed to a concrete bunker behind him. "Several dozen. We found more behind the building."

"Lots more." Carlos's voice was grave. Even the boy who was never serious was freaked.

She stepped closer to the stone, crouched down, and brushed it clean.

"Ofelia Gutiérrez." She read it out loud, then gasped, leaping up and putting her hands to her mouth. "Abuelita!"

Lupe ran over to her. "Marisol! That was your grandmother?"

Marisol shook her head. "No, no. Abuelita is that old woman in Yabucoa in the senior center I mentioned. She . . ." She took a deep breath, remembering as she was talking. "She told me that her abuela was on Vieques, that she was angry. Abuelita is a nickname, her real name is Ofelia Gutiérrez. She said they left her alone here. . . ." She looked back down at the stone. "But Abuelita is, like, eighty-something, so her grandmother is long dead. . . ."

Then she registered the date. "September thirteen, 1928?"

Sam nodded. "That's what the death date is on all of these."

Marisol's throat tightened. "That was the date of the last category five hurricane in Puerto Rico. San Felipe II. It killed over three hundred people."

Everyone froze where they were, eyes wide, staring at each other, then at the stones.

Javier's voice was low and quiet. "The resort dug up this area to build this storage building. But there was another partially built structure here before."

Lupe broke in. "Marisol, didn't Jones say that the navy started to build a munitions storage on what would be protected land?"

Marisol just nodded. "That was right before they declared it a nature preserve and left not long after." She swallowed. "Jones said because of the ghosts."

Lupe's head snapped up to look at Marisol. "You don't think . . . they dug up the graveyard of the Vieques residents who were killed in the hurricane, do you?"

Marisol nodded again, numb. "That would explain why the ghosts were seen back then."

Sam added, as if in a trance, "And when the resort corporation built this storage structure, they dug up even more." He dropped the tombstone he'd been holding and began to retch.

"Well, I guess we know why your friend's abuela is pissed," Carlos said as he looked around.

"They left her here, she said. So, she died thirteen years before the navy threw her family off the island and relocated them to St. Croix."

Javier walked over to them. "They dug up Abuelita—" He gestured around him. "And the rest of them?"

Pieces were clicking together in Marisol's brain. "So, when they took her family away, they left her grave here on the island." She pointed to the stone on the ground in front of her. "And now they've desecrated her grave. Again."

"Seems like it." Lupe put her fingertips to her skull as if to soothe it from the dark news.

Still kneeling on the ground, Sam spat, wiped his mouth, and then said, "And it's my father's fault." His voice was shaky.

"Actually, it's the navy's," Marisol said in an angry tone. "They were taking over the land and were the first to dig this area up, so they're the ones who woke them."

"Woke them?" Sam's voice was thin and reedy.

"Yes. Woke them."

Lupe turned to Javier. "This military guy, Jones, tried to tell his superiors, but they didn't believe him. Then I bet the entire platoon, or whatever, was haunted and they pulled off the island altogether."

Javier's eyes widened. "Wait, they knew what they'd done. That's why they made it a nature preserve. They tried to cover it up."

Lupe shrugged. "Maybe they succeeded. Jones said it was quiet until a few months ago. The ghosts were at rest, I guess."

"Until my father and his greedy friends disturbed them again."

Marisol nodded at Sam, then said, "But I think Lupe's right. I'm just not convinced they're the ones killing people and taking their hearts. Jones said nothing like that happened when they were around before."

Carlos pointed to the stones they'd unearthed. "And there are women and children among them. Not exactly ghoul material."

"That means the killer's still out there," Javier responded.

Lupe nodded. "*And* the ghosts."

Then they all stayed there staring at the stones, not saying anything. The noise from the nearby event grounds seemed suddenly mocking and forced. A microphone squealed to life and a voice said, "Test, test, test."

Carlos jolted. "Shit! I'm supposed to be onstage!" He spun around and indicated the macabre mess around them. "But what are we going to do?"

Javier put his hands on his friend's shoulders. "Go, Carlos. We'll find Lupe's uncle and call in the cavalry. You need to go on as if all is fine, so we don't have a panic. Go!"

Carlos nodded at Javier and the rest of them and took off running back toward the grounds.

Sam was still kneeling and staring at the ground. "We have to stop him."

"Who? Carlos?"

Sam shook his head. "No, my father. This isn't right. This ugly resort, this whole thing. It's just not right."

"Yeah, no shit." Javier scowled.

Javier really didn't like this Sam guy, but Marisol could tell he was as horrified as the rest of them. And here they were, with no plan and hordes of people arriving on the island.

Never a dull moment with this group.

Why couldn't she get normal friends?

Chapter Twenty-five

Lupe

JAVIER'S SARCASTIC COMMENT to Sam was not lost on Lupe. She put her hands on her hips and shot Javier a look. "Really? *Now* you're going to be snippy and petty?"

Javier scowled at her. At Sam. At the trees. Boy was always scowling these days. "Let's find your uncle." He shoved his hands deep into his jeans pockets and started stalking back toward the resort. Marisol and Lupe shared a look. Sam seemed distracted. He reached out for Lupe's arm.

"I gotta go. We're going to need more than some tombstones to prove this."

"True, but we're going to find it together. Let's go talk to my uncle." She started to walk away but he grabbed her arm again. Why did boys insist on doing that? It *so* pissed her off.

"What? Sam, what?"

"I need to go."

This stopped her. "Excuse me?"

"I have to check on something. I just thought of some documents my father has on his computer that might help. I know where he keeps his passwords." His eyes were wide and heavy, like there were weights on each lid, each shoulder.

What the hell? "Documents? What kind of documents?"

Silence, then, "I can't tell you, it's better if I just show you. If I show everyone."

She stared at him for a minute. Was Sam a coward? She had patience for a lot of things, but not cowardice. "I think it's best if we stay together."

"Look, Lupe." His eyes were more focused, like he'd just decided on something. "I think this is why I'm here."

"What do you mean?"

"I think this is what I have to offer to the story, what I bring to the party. I understand this world, my father's world." When he said the word "father" he had a look on his face like he'd smelled something bad.

"But what documents?"

He just kissed her forehead. "You're just going to have to trust me."

She didn't *have* to do anything, and she didn't trust easily, but weirdly she trusted this rich boy she'd only known for a few days. She nodded. "Okay."

"Thank you," he whispered, and then he was gone, cutting through the brush, running to the front of the building toward the parking lot.

The day was only getting weirder.

Marisol had turned around when she noticed Lupe wasn't next to her. "What's wrong? Where's the white boy going?"

"Sam! His name is Sam!" Lupe yelled, and was immediately sorry. But she suddenly felt stupid for trusting him. "And I don't know."

Veterinary school. When they'd spent that afternoon touring the resort, Sam had told her he was studying to be a vet. Someone who would know how to cut up a body. Was she being a naïve idiot? Lupe swallowed hard.

She and Marisol continued in silence, walking on either side of the row of stones. Now that they knew what they were, it seemed sacrilegious to tread on them. They reached the patio to find Javier and an older man in a baseball cap yelling at each other.

"You took off for several hours yesterday, Utierre! I can't have my staff taking off randomly during the day the job is due to be completed!"

"I told you, it was important!"

In a moment of supremely shitty timing, Lupe and Marisol arrived just then at the edge of the conversation. The contractor looked at them with a smirk and looked back at Javier. "Sure, 'important.'"

Marisol put her hands on her hips in classic Lupe superhero pose. "And what are you implying? He was not doing anything untoward–"

"You're fired," the man said to Javier, and started walking away.

Javier's hands dropped by his sides. "What?"

He turned around but continued walking away. "I'm done with you, Utierre. Get your shit and get off the property."

"But—"

"Now!" And he stalked off, disappearing around the corner of the building.

Great. That's all the guy needed. He needed that job. She felt totally powerless.

"Javier." Lupe's voice seemed to startle him; he jumped and seemed to realize she and Marisol were standing there. "Maybe Sam can do something." It was the only thing she could think of to suggest.

Javier looked around. "Where is he?"

Oh, right. "He . . . had to go do something."

Javier through up his hands. "Great. The one time I actually need him, and he takes off. He's probably scared."

"That's not true!" Her voice had sharp edges, mainly because she had wondered the exact same thing and that bothered her. "He's . . . getting some proof to help."

Javier laughed and looked at her with a bitter smile. "Some proof. Is that what he told you?" He stared at her for a beat, and it wasn't the kind of stare that made her feel good. "What is it with you two, anyway?"

This made the heat rise behind Lupe's face. "There is nothing *with* us two. He's a friend, that's all." Why did he keep bringing this up? She'd waited all winter to see him and it had all been going wrong, almost from the beginning.

Javier looked at her. "I thought *I* was your friend."

"Don't be ridiculous, Javier. You're more than a friend and you know it."

His voice got quieter, hurt edging each word. "Then why did you stop talking with me after the hurricane?'

"What are you talking about? We talked almost every day."

"Yeah, about me, about the island. You stopped sharing anything about you."

Lupe glanced at Marisol. Perhaps she'd been right. She'd shut him out, too. "I'm sorry, I was trying—"

"Lupe!" There was no mistaking the foghorn of that voice. Her uncle was standing in all his dress-uniform glory near the front of the building. "Utierre, Marisol, come here!" He swiped at them impatiently as if they were dust bunnies under the bed, and they weren't stupid: they ran to him like they were on a string.

The conversation with Javier was going to have to wait.

The limousines had been arriving since around three. A line of them as far as the eye could see led to the front entrance of the resort, and Lupe had to wonder how the hell they'd gotten all those monster vehicles across the strip of water where the

Caribbean Sea meets the Atlantic Ocean. But given the VIP level, there were probably private yachts involved.

Protestors streamed in and out among the limos, from the direction of the public ferries, carrying signs that read KEEP YOUR HANDS OFF OUR LANDS! and VIEQUES IS NOT FOR SALE! and her personal favorite, I'LL TELL YOU WHERE TO SHOVE YOUR PAPER TOWELS! with a less than flattering cartoon image of the president. Handling either of these groups was bad enough, but managing the two clashing with each other and an evening's worth of activities? Her uncle had his hands full.

And his job depended on it. Literally.

His staff was stationed all over the grounds trying to both blend in *and* lend a sense of comfort, given the recent events. They'd tried their best to keep the news under wraps, but with the wonder of the internet, word got out. ZOMBIES INVADE VIEQUES! and EL CUCO RETURNS? the headlines blared. Her uncle had stationed himself near the grandstand where the bigwigs would be sitting, and where the captain was likely to be. There was nothing concrete pointing to the captain, but he was the most likely suspect so far. Her uncle didn't agree with that yet, but she would keep an eye on him anyway.

Marisol appeared at Lupe's left, and they nodded at each other like spies in a television series. But given how helpless she was feeling, and the events of the day, it was more like a horror movie.

"My uncle says they're all on the island now, the VIPs. It's only a matter of getting them all through the protestors, on the grounds, and seated before the festivities begin."

Marisol looked back at the line of limos that still hadn't moved, the crowds of protestors weaving in and out of the stopped vehicles, yelling into the tinted windows. "At this rate that should be around midnight."

Javier walked up and stood on her other side. She could feel the stress coming off him as he stood super straight. Great, a nice topping of tension.

All three of them looked at the swelling crowd while her uncle talked with random staff. Javier sighed. "If this is all coming to a head tonight, it's bound to be a dumpster fire."

"Yeah, if dumpster fires included ghosts, heart-stealing murderers, and crooked politicians."

"Don't they all?" Marisol added. "Sounds like a typical Friday night for this group."

Javier snorted. "Yeah, I think someone's human heart gift to Lupe was enough horror for one week."

"Thank you! Tell this girl she needs to tell her uncle before the psycho finds her in real life." Marisol crossed her arms and glared at Lupe.

"Real life? Don't you think putting one in her backpack was enough?"

Marisol's eyes widened. "Excuse me?" She wheeled on Lupe.

Lupe shrugged. "Oops! Forgot to tell you."

"For someone who talks so much, you certainly are leaving out a lot of details lately!"

Javier jumped in. "You're telling me!"

Lupe put her hands out. "Look. I know, and I'm sorry, guys. I love you both, and I'm sorry I held back so much over the last few months, but I really was trying to just be there for you."

"But that's it, 'just.' We want to be there for you, too."

Lupe reached out and pulled Marisol into a hug. Javier made a sarcastic "aww" behind them, and Marisol pulled back and shook her finger in Lupe's face. "But you should have told me about the damn heart in your bag!"

Out of the corner of her eye, Lupe saw movement nearby.

The captain had appeared next to the grandstand and was checking his watch nervously. "Guys, look," she whispered, pointing toward the police captain. "You might be right, Javier. He sure looks like he's up to no good." The captain looked around and skirted the building's edge toward the back.

Lupe looked at her uncle, but he was going over a map of the property with a few of his officers. She started to follow the captain herself, but Javier put his hand out. "I'll go."

She gave him the look.

Javier put his hands up. "I know the grounds and the building better than you two, and we need to have someone out here where the action is. Besides, no one left a human heart in my bag!"

"Wait, weren't you fired?"

He smiled. "Right, so I have nothing to lose!"

"Yeah, but I think we should stick—"

"Lupe!" her uncle bellowed from mere feet away.

She jumped rather comically. Was the yelling necessary? But now was not the time. "¿Sí, Tío?"

"Get me my extra radio from the truck. This one's dead." He held up the offending device, then chucked the keys toward her, which she caught with no problem.

"10-4, Chief!" Lupe turned to Javier. "Guess it is you; be careful, Javi. Text us if you find anything or you need help. And not a word to Tío!"

He nodded and started off, but she grabbed his arm this time, made sure her uncle was distracted, pulled him back to her, and gave him a full, open-mouthed kiss. When she let go of his arm and leaned back, a huge grin spread across his face, and he basically skipped off.

Lupe put her arm through Marisol's. "C'mon. Walk me to the truck."

Side by side they made their way through the crowd, heading for her uncle's familiar, beaten-up truck in the distance. Tired of being chauffeured around, he'd brought it back with him on the ferry the day before.

They broke free of the mass of the crowd, and as she walked, Lupe stared at her feet. "Mari, I'm sorry." Her voice was quiet but determined.

"For what?"

"That I wasn't . . . available in the right way when you were dealing with the hurricane and . . . after."

Marisol waved her hand in dismissal. "No, Lupe. I don't know how I would have made it through without your family. You were just doing what you thought was best."

"But it had the opposite effect! Dad and I, we felt so helpless up there in Vermont. We're sitting on our deck, the leaves changing around the lake, and you guys were dealing with hell on earth. But Esteban didn't want us to come down. He said he'd just have to worry about us, too, that he felt better knowing we were safe in Vermont."

"And I don't blame him!" Marisol barked. Then she laughed. "I'm surprised you didn't hop on a plane anyway!"

"I tried! I was just about to press Book Ticket on the website when Dad appeared over my shoulder and took his credit card away from me!"

Marisol laughed harder now, and Lupe couldn't help but join in. Protestors walking by shot them nasty looks. Not the circumstances for laughter, but that only made it harder to hold back.

They arrived at the car with their arms around each other's shoulders, tears rolling down their cheeks. Lupe took her arm back to get the keys from her pocket and pressed the fob, the truck beeping at her in response. She opened the front passenger door.

"Just an FYI, my uncle's kind of a slob with his truck—"

But whatever she was about to say left in a *whoosh* when she looked in the passenger seat. *Her* seat, when she rode with her tío.

There, pinned to the tan upholstered back, was another heart. Or was it the same one from her backpack? What difference did it make? The message was clear. Lupe swallowed deeply.

"Lupe, what's up? Is something wr—"

Lupe stepped back while Marisol fully took in the sight. Drying blood trailed down below the heart like arteries connecting it to the seat, and the air of the truck smelled hot and salty, leaving a metallic taste on her tongue. It was then she saw the bit of a knife handle that was extending from the center of the organ, an arrow that reached out to pierce Lupe and Marisol.

"Mari . . . isn't that . . . your brother's knife?" The yellow skulls on the handle were worn, but still bright.

Marisol nodded, her mouth hanging open.

Lupe thought back to last summer. "Wait, didn't I kick that down a sewer drain when we fought last year?"

Marisol swallowed, hard. "I had a guy fish it out for me." She looked at Lupe with big eyes. "It was all I had left of him."

"Where do you keep it?"

Marisol pulled her backpack around, the sound of zippers whizzing like bees. "I keep it . . . in this side pocket. . . ." But her fingers searched in vain, and they both knew it wasn't there.

"Someone took it from your bag."

"But when? I've had it on me since I got off the ferry . . . except for when we went to talk to the lieutenant colonel."

Someone had followed them and taken the knife.

Marisol grabbed Lupe's sleeve. "Do you think someone is trying to frame me?"

"I doubt it's that well thought out. I mean, you weren't

here until today, and the other hearts were taken earlier." She looked back at the gruesome sight on her uncle's truck seat. "Nah, I think this was a message to me."

"A message about what?"

"To stop digging into things, I imagine."

Marisol stared. "Point taken."

"As if! All this does is make me more determined to find out who it is."

Marisol smiled at her. "Now that's the Lupe I know and am irritated by! So, we going to tell your uncle?"

"Not yet." Lupe chewed her lower lip.

"What? Why not? Lupe, Facebook posts are one thing, but this is serious shit!"

"Mari, it's been nonstop serious shit. But if my uncle doesn't solve this case before the opening, the governor is going to fire him!"

"What? Are you serious? After all he's done for this island? More than the damn governor's done, let me tell you!"

"I know, but do you see why I can't tell him yet? He needs to stay focused on keeping all these people safe, not on these messages to me. He has to keep his job, being a cop is all he's ever wanted since he was, like, nine years old!" Lupe reached gingerly over the passenger seat and grabbed the beat-up radio from between the seats.

"Okay, okay! But we have to stick together, nena. After all my physical labor this summer, I can be your bodyguard." She flexed her muscles.

Lupe smiled. "I feel safer already."

Truth was, she did. It was nice to have someone have your back.

Chapter Twenty-six

Javier

JAVIER HAD STAYED several yards behind, so the captain wouldn't know he was following, as he had snuck around the back of the building and made his way to the basement. Javier entered the silent stairwell and pressed himself against the wall like he had seen in the movies, stifling a cough from the cloud of white sheetrock dust that engulfed him as he moved. The odor of fresh paint and cement was heavy in the air, and he had to admit he'd always liked that smell. It smelled like newness and . . . possibility.

He padded down the stairs, and was trying to decide which way to go when the sound of footsteps came toward him from the left. He ducked into a small closet space. The captain rushed by and up the stairs, out of breath. Javier waited until he was certain the man was not coming back, then stepped out. He was about to run up the stairs and keep following the captain when the sound of something falling came from the way the captain had come. Curious, he decided to follow it and find out what he had been up to in the empty basement. But the only things he found were bags of dried cement and paint cans.

"This is a waste of time," he said out loud, and was about to turn around when he saw a light coming from the far storage room. He made his way toward the light, careful in case someone else was around. He peeked around the corner and didn't see anyone there. Once in the room, he discovered a lighted table covered with electrical parts and pieces, a clay-like substance, and a white powder. He put a bit on his finger and smelled it: fertilizer. It was a makeshift worktable, a door over two sawhorses, but not for any work he knew that was going on at the resort. He took out his phone and took a photo of the odd collection of items, then made his way quietly back to the stairwell. He took the steps two at a time, and carefully peered around the basement door. There was no sign of the captain around the building, so he ran to the front to find the chief. He found him standing near the bandstand with Hernán.

"Chief Dávila! There's something I need to show you." He turned to Hernán. "Excuse me." He turned his back on the captain's son and pulled up the photo on his phone. He said to the chief in a whisper, "I found this in a room in the basement. It isn't anything the resort is working on, so it seemed suspicious."

The chief peered at the phone. "Help an old man out and zoom into that part of the photo, will you, Utierre? I want to see the labels."

Javier obliged, enlarging the pic.

The chief's head snapped up. His expression still looked calm and collected, but Javier could see concern around his eyes.

"Where did you say this was?"

"A room in the basement of the main building."

"Whatever was being made there is done and gone. But it's not good."

Hernán asked, "Not good how?"

"Javier, did you see anyone down there?"

Javier glanced over at Hernán and paused. The officer seemed to be eavesdropping, but he was going to learn the truth about his father soon, so it might as well be now. "Yes. Captain Torres. He was down there alone before I found it."

Hernán's eyes widened. "I was just telling the chief that my father's been acting weird lately."

Dávila grabbed his radio and barked, "Ramirez, get the bomb squad over here near the grandstand, stat! I need them to sweep the area."

Bomb?

Chapter Twenty-seven

Lupe

💀

LUPE AND MARISOL were shaken by what they found in the truck, but they put their game faces on and slipped among the crowd like minnows, bobbing and weaving through the mass of humanity.

They arrived to find Javier and Hernán standing around Chief Dávila like schoolchildren, the look in their eyes holding helplessness. Even Esteban seemed restless.

"So, what'd we miss?"

Marisol snorted, but coughed to cover it up. Lupe shot her a look.

The three men filled them in on what had transpired. Her uncle had sent one officer to find Captain Torres, but he hadn't returned yet. They didn't know for a fact it was him yet, and he wanted the bulk of the force here, on the event grounds.

Of course, Lupe wasn't surprised that the elder Torres looked like the culprit. And after their little car ride, she knew he hated her enough to stab a heart through her car seat. Lupe looked at Hernán with empathy. "I'm sorry about your father, Hernán."

The young officer looked at her, his eyes glassy. "He isn't a kind man, my father. Especially not to me. But I always tried to make him proud anyway, you know?"

She nodded. "I do know." She knew what it was like to have parents who disappointed you, though her father was trying really hard to straighten up.

For a moment they all watched the comings and goings, the crowd swelling, increasing with each ferry's arrival, the staff hustling around, preparing the event. The police skirted the edges, equally as helpless.

An officer came to the edge of the bandstand and called the chief over. She whispered something in his ear. Esteban came back to the group. "Where's Sam?" he asked. "His father is looking for him."

"He went to get a document or something that he thinks will help," Lupe offered.

Javier sneered. "Document. How will a piece of paper help? We need people willing to fight, not . . . Coward."

Lupe turned to him. "Actually, if you paid attention in history class, documents are at the heart of any significant change in history since humans could write!"

"Well, he should be here. His father started this entire thing, after all, and—"

"He is not the same as his father! You of all people should—"

"Children!" Esteban's bark made them both jump and silence fell over their group. Except for Marisol's quiet snickering at his chastising. She sure was having a good time.

"Tío, they're going to try to privatize all the beaches!"

"What? No, that's not possible."

"But it is! I think that's part of what Sam is trying to prove—"

The radio crackled to life, and a voice came out of the small speaker. "Um, excuse me—"

"Quiet!" But he wasn't saying that because he was trying to listen to the radio. "Do you hear that?" Esteban was leaning forward, head tilted, listening to . . . the now-full audience?

Lupe listened but could only hear the murmur of the crowd . . . but then she heard something else. They all seemed to hear it now, a shushing, whispering sound on the wind.

The radio squawked. "Chief? I think we've got a problem."

And another voice broke in. "Um, Chief? You're not going to believe this."

Voices overlapping, reports from all edges of the property. Dávila grabbed on to the side of the grandstand and swung himself up, climbing to the highest step.

"Tío!" Lupe called up in a loud stage whisper. She didn't know why she was bothering to whisper when they were surrounded by thousands of people. "What do you see?"

Esteban stood up tall, his eyes wide. He swung down and spoke into the radio. "Is that what I think it is?"

Squawk. "Yep. I can see dozens of them. Maybe hundreds! And they're . . . glowing."

"Here, too. And transparent."

The third voice just started reciting the Lord's Prayer in Spanish.

The radio silenced as the chief pressed the Talk button. "What are they doing?"

A silent beat, then. "They're just . . . walking."

"Walking where?"

Another silent beat.

A crackle.

Finally, a shaky voice broke in.

"Toward the event."

Chapter Twenty-eight

Javier

"JESUS." CHIEF DÁVILA called his staff toward him, giving them directions to spread out. His voice was low, but Javier could make out what he was saying. "We have to find the bomb before those ghosts get here. When the crowd sees them, it will be total chaos." He turned to Javier, "Son, could you lead an officer through that maze of a basement to where you found those materials? See if there is anything else in that basement that might give us a clue as to what's being planned and where? I'll send one of my officers with you, but I need someone I can trust. In the meantime, I've got to convince these people to evacuate the bandstand without causing a panic. They're arguing with my officers. Arguing!" The chief seemed uncharacteristically flustered.

Hernán stepped forward. "Chief, if it's all right with you, I'd like to go with Javier."

Dávila just looked at the young patrolman.

"I know what you're thinking, he's my father, but that's exactly why I want to go. He has been acting weird lately, and I think he needs our help. My help."

Dávila looked at him for a moment, then nodded. "Come right back. The events are due to begin at eight p.m. sharp."

Both nodded and headed back around the building toward the rear entrance to the basement. As they passed the entrance to the private beach, (Javier was never going to get used to calling it that—island beaches were not supposed to be private) Hernán stopped.

"Wait. I think I saw someone near the water."

Javier squinted, but the setting sun lengthened the shadows. "Who?"

"I don't know, but it might have been my father."

"The boat!"

"What?"

"Last night I saw your father pulling a boat into the trees."

Hernán paused, then said, "I'm going to check it out, I'll meet you in the basement."

Javier nodded and ignored the burning in the pit of his stomach. He made his way back to the stairs' entrance. The longer shadows made sneaking easier. The stairwell lights were off, and he decided not to turn them on and alert the captain, if he was down there, to his presence. His sneakers made no sound as he made his way down the hallway, stopping just outside of the small room where he'd found the makeshift workbench. He stood there breathing for a moment, and was considering waiting for Hernán when he noticed the mumbling sound. He listened closely. . . . It was praying, the Hail Mary in Spanish.

Praying?

He peeked his head carefully around the corner and saw the captain standing over the table, his head bobbing, the prayer tumbling from his lips like drops of water. Javier stepped around the corner, quietly. He wondered if it was wise to think it, but nothing about the captain seemed threatening at the moment. In fact, he felt a pang of pity: the man looked sad and alone.

As if sensing Javier's presence, the captain spun around

and saw Javier's form standing in the shadow of the doorway. "Who's there? Hernán? Is that you?" The hum of thousands of voices and the tinny sound of piped-in music pressed in from the outside, but in the still basement, his voice was clear and loud.

Javier stepped forward. "No, sir. It's Javier Utierre. The chief sent me."

"Oh." The man seemed disappointed and not the least bit alarmed.

"Did . . . did you set this up?" Javier asked, indicating the table of bomb-making equipment.

The captain spun around as if he'd already forgotten Javier was there. "What? No. No, of course not."

Javier wondered if he was lying. He had to find out what was planned. He stepped closer, wondering again if it was a wise choice, knowing it really wasn't. "Captain Torres, can you tell me what's going on here? Is something bad going to happen at the event?" He looked at his phone out of reflex. The concert started in ten minutes. They were almost out of time. As he waited for the man to answer, he realized he didn't have a clue how to approach this. Why hadn't he paid more attention in psychology class?

"Yes, I think something bad is going to happen." He picked up the remnants of a clock and turned around to face Javier.

He thinks?

Javier stepped up until he was only a few feet from the captain, and as he did, the man's eyes shot up. Had he made a mistake? Was Torres a serial killer and going to attack him?

"I found the boat, and the unconscious officer," the captain said. "I've suspected what you were doing for weeks now, suspected what you were. But I didn't want to believe it, so I tried to protect you. But I was wrong, and I'm going to stop you, I have to," he whispered into the still air of the room.

Javier had no clue how to handle this. He coughed, then said, "Sir, I saw *you* with the boat. I haven't 'done' anything, and I don't need protecting—"

Then there was an explosion, the sound ringing off everything in the basement, and Javier reflexively put his hands over his ears and bent over with the pain in his head. Had it happened? Had the bomb gone off? Was he too late? He looked up at Captain Torres and saw his face was pulled down in shock, his glazed eyes staring over Javier's shoulder, a dark stain spreading on his crisp uniform shirt.

What?

What was happening?

Javier was about to spin around and look behind him when something struck the back of his skull, and suddenly the basement floor was rising to meet him.

Chapter Twenty-nine

Marisol

THEY COULD TELL the minute the crowd of ghosts met the
event crowd. There were choruses of gasps, then screams, then
waves of panicked movement. Complete chaos was coming
their way. Marisol could feel the burn of anxiety rising from
her belly. Since the hurricane she had been in so many situations and crowds, protesting for those left homeless, and the
feeling of being in the center of an emotionally elevated crowd
was becoming way too familiar. It was a sense of complete and
total helplessness in the middle of earth-shattering disaster.
And here it was again, like an unwanted guest. Just throw in
supernatural elements and a human threat and you got today.

Even though they were outside, it was like the air had been
sucked out of the space. She longed to just step away toward
the beach for a moment and catch her breath. She looked over
in that direction and saw a uniformed figure in the main building's shadow.

Wait, wasn't that the captain's son? Hernán? Where was Javier? Hadn't they left together?

Marisol turned to tell Lupe, but her friend was engulfed in

the maelstrom that surrounded her uncle. As she knew from her volunteer work, strong leadership in these kinds of situations was crucial. And if anyone could get them all through this nightmare it was Lupe's uncle. She looked back and saw Hernán moving across the grassy expanse, toward the shore.

He was totally up to something.

She rushed over, leaving the bedlam behind her, and her breathing started to come in normally. It felt good to be free of the crowd's push and she liked having something to do.

She followed him to the back, working to keep sight of him in the dark. There was some ambient light from the festivities, but not enough to see by. She caught sight of him skulking over to the beach and pulling a small boat from a hiding place in the brush toward the water. And a sea launch with no witnesses.

Except her!

But wait . . . He was pulling something else back into the brush. Was that . . . a body? Could that be Javier?

Oh *hell* no.

She took off in a stealthy run and got to the beach just as he pushed the tip of the boat into the water. She jumped and threw her body on him, tumbling them both over the canoe and tackling him to the ground. He was not all that much bigger than she was, slight and not very tall, and she had been working very hard, but he was a professional with a gun at his hip and she had to move fast.

Hernán was stunned for a second, but then he came to life and started punching at Marisol, and they became a tangle of limbs and fists. He might be trained in hand-to-hand combat, but she was strong now.

And she knew how to fight dirty.

She brought her knee up to his crotch, but he managed to maneuver away so that all her knee met was air. He used that chance to roll them around on the sand until he was on top, trying to pin her arms down. She was a pinwheel of arms and legs and she managed to get him off her enough that she could make a fist and pull it back.

She punched him in the jaw, and his head flew back with a spray of spit and blood. As she brought her fist back again, he reached around and grabbed her hair, yanking her backward. She felt as if patches of flesh had been ripped off her skull, but she worked to regain her control. But with the hair move, he got the upper hand again and pinned her once more to the sand, his knees on either shoulder, his other hand on her throat, and as he squeezed, the stars started to dance behind her eyelids. She tried to swallow, tried to take a breath, but there was no room in her throat to get the air through. What she was seeing became more stars, so much more that they were crowding out her sight, and she wondered if she was going to die on that beach.

As difficult as her life had been, she wanted desperately to see her friends again.

To help the people of the island.

To live.

Chapter Thirty

Javier

JAVIER STAGGERED DOWN the near-dark basement hall, feeling the wall hand over hand in hopes it would lead him out. He basically fell up the stairs, his brain barely able to get his beaten body to move, a deep throbbing in his head making him grateful for the dark. It was too much like when he used to wake up the morning after getting high, when it felt as if the drugs had yanked out parts of his insides, leaving behind raw, throbbing wounds. Yeah, he'd rather skip that feeling. It wasn't as if he needed a reminder of why he'd gotten clean.

I'm only doing what you wanted. You told me again and again that the gringos took the heart of the island, and you seemed to hate them for it.

A weak voice, watery sounding. *No, you misunderstood. I don't hate anyone.* A rattling cough. *And it was you that took my heart, you that broke it.*

Very poetic, old man. I just did what you couldn't, what you didn't have the guts to do.

Was this a conversation that had happened while he was passed out? While Captain Torres died? But how would he remember it? No, it had to be a dream he'd had while he was knocked out on the floor. But if it was a dream, what had actually happened?

He worked to slow his breathing and prepared to head back into the crowd. But before he took another step, he saw movement in the greenery on the far side of the resort property, and a glowing blue light illuminating the undersides of the palm fronds.

He knew that light.

They were coming.

Hand on his head, he staggered back toward the grandstand and his friends. He had to get to the chief and tell him what was going on. But as he walked, it was as if he were on a ship, the ground bucking and swaying, and he thought he was going to puke. He pushed forward and heard the chaos before he saw it. The hum of the crowd had become screams, the mass of people pressing backward toward the building and the grandstand of VIPs. Someone was calling for calm on a loudspeaker, but it was having no effect. Javier could see the blue light flooding the edges of the event area like water, pushing against the crowd, the empty eyes of the ghosts boring into them.

He heard Dávila before he saw him, so he threw himself in that direction. He must have looked bad, because the first policeman he came across stepped aside and let him walk through to the chief without a question. That's when Javier put his hand in front of his face and saw the blood.

"Jesus Christ, Utierre, are you all right?" Lupe's uncle took him by the arms and looked into his eyes, probably searching for signs of concussion since he clearly had suffered a head wound.

"A little dizzy, but I'm all right. Chief, I think it was Hernán!"

"What? The captain's son?"

"Yes! He shot his father right in front of me, then knocked me out. I think he put a bomb in the grandstand."

"No, impossible. The bomb squad has swept the entire area and found nothing."

Lupe appeared at his side. "Javi! What happened?" She started fussing over him. Even through the pain, he kind of liked it.

A young officer came up to the chief, her hands shaking slightly as she held up her smartphone. "Chief, you're going to want to take this."

Javier expected him to tell her now wasn't the time, but something in how or what she said seemed to make him realize he had to take it. He held the phone up to his head.

"No, sir, it's a FaceTime call, from La Salle."

"What? Like, a video?"

Her gaze caught Javier's and she fought off a small smile. "Yes, sir."

Esteban held up the phone. "La Salle, you there?"

A man's face appeared on the phone, the image distorted as he held it in front of him as he walked. "Yeah, Chief. I was patrolling the village of Isabel Segunda as you asked, and a neighbor tipped me off on some weird goings-on around this house." The camera swung around, and an abandoned house surrounded by beat-up metal fencing appeared on-screen.

"I know that house!" Lupe yelled. "It's across the street from where old man Carter was killed."

La Salle's voice again, narrating what was on the screen. "You're right." The camera swooped again, and now a dilapidated little house appeared.

"He owned half the island and that's where he chose to live? Damn." Javier realized after he said it that the timing for that comment was probably bad, but the chief didn't even seem to notice.

"Get to the point, La Salle. We're kind of busy here."

Javier snorted. This time he earned a look from the chief.

The camera started moving around the fence and into the darkened interior of the one-story concrete home. "It's in here that the weird shi—stuff is."

The interior of the house was fairly dark, the only light a bare bulb in the corner, but as the camera lens adjusted, it came into focus. It was an empty room, with a single bare mattress in one corner and a small sink in the other. "Someone's been staying here, but look at this . . ."

The image swung again—it was kind of dizzying—and then a flag came into view. A Puerto Rican flag. Javier was about to ask what was so important about that when the blue triangle that should contain the star appeared. In the center of it was a patch of an anatomically correct heart, sewed in place.

"Madre de Dios," the chief said under his breath.

Lupe's eyes grew wide. "Tío! That's why he got to the crime scene so quickly!"

"Who?"

"Hernán." Then she stopped, her head whipping around. "Wait, where's Marisol?"

An officer standing next to them leaned in. "The dark-haired girl who was with you? I saw her over that way with Torres." He pointed toward the beach and then turned back to what he was doing.

"The captain?" Lupe and Esteban said at the same time.

"No, Hernán."

Lupe and her uncle took off, running at top speed toward the back, leaving Javier and his aching head standing there in shock.

Chapter Thirty-one

Marisol

MARISOL WAS DREAMING of her mother. Well, not really dreaming, but in that twilight before unconsciousness she could see her. Not in the exhausted and wasted state she was in before she died, but rather the stylish, edgy version of her youth. Her face was floating above Marisol's, dark curls cascading on either side like curtains. Her mother was trying to get her up for school, but Marisol couldn't get her limbs to work. She tried to say so, but her thoughts wouldn't come out of her mouth. Then the hair shimmered and changed color to blond and Lupe's face was above hers. That's when Marisol realized Dream Lupe was shaking her, yelling "Get up!" in Marisol's face. Then she was rising, the surface of consciousness closer and closer above her head until she burst through, saw Hernán above her, his pale face red and twisted in exertion and hatred. She felt the burning pressure around her throat and remembered.

He seemed surprised to see her revived, so she took that opportunity to shove him off with her knees, pushing him backward into the sand. She punched him across the jaw, a loud *crunch* echoing and a spray of blood flying as she wound up for another. She was going to beat him across his face until he passed out, then she might keep beating him, until . . .

Wait.

Years under El Cuco's curse, her homeland ravaged by storm and forgotten, Marisol understood anger. But this guy . . . he was trying to kill hundreds of people. Didn't he deserve to die? Regardless, she needed to know the answer to one question.

"Why?" she bellowed into his face, pulling him up by the shirt.

Hernán moved his jaw from side to side, blood spread across his cheek, trailing into his hair. "You, of all people, should understand! They're ruining this island!"

"Me, of all people?"

"I looked you up. You're an activist. You know what they're doing to our island? Like my father always said, they're taking the heart of our island! He didn't have the guts to do anything about it, but I do!" His eyes were almost spinning in his head. "They needed to pay!" Spittle gathered on his lips.

"Just who is 'they' in your tiny mind?"

"The gringos! The colonizers!"

"What, like your mother?"

His face grew even darker. "If I could expunge all my mother's blood from my veins, I would! She . . . well, you can't imagine the things she did to me."

Marisol laughed. "Oh, I bet I can! You're not the only one who had a difficult childhood, pendejo! And you're not killing just the gringos with this violence! There are thousands of Puerto Ricans, many from right here on Vieques, out there! You ripped the hearts out of half a dozen people, you psychopath!"

"Sacrifices must be made. And you can't tell me that you

don't think they deserved it! Each of those people was selfish and greedy and you know it."

"Yeah, I do know it. But did they deserve to die?"

"Yes!"

"Maybe, but you can't be the one to decide that! Who are you to be judge, jury, and executioner?" She saw the weird glow from his eyes, his expression getting stranger as they spoke. She knew that look. If the heart ripping wasn't enough, this would prove her supposition: this dude was pure evil. But she needed a new strategy. She needed to find out where the bomb was.

"They did deserve to die, you're right." She nodded as if she agreed. "So, you put the bomb in the audience. Garbage can?"

He scoffed. Amazing he could still be arrogant while being held down by a girl who weighed 110 pounds soaking wet. "Of course not. I'm not a savage!"

She laughed. She couldn't help it. "So you'd want to put it where you'd get the maximum impact. Bet they won't find anything under the grandstand. You must have been too smart for them."

He smiled, seemingly grateful that someone finally appreciated his plan. "It was really so simple! The grandstand is made up of hundreds of metal tubes. A strategic placement right in the middle will be the most effective at obliterating as many targets as possible. Those seats will be filled with men in power, men who are destroying our island for their financial gain!"

"Oh, like your great-grandfather?"

A look of confusion clouded Hernán's eyes.

"You see, I looked *you* up, too, Hernán Torres. Your paternal great-grandfather brokered the damn deal to sell off the island piece by piece after the last category-five hurricane. According to your standards, colonizer blood runs through your veins from both parents! God, all this violence to get back at the colonizers, and you *are* the colonizer!"

A beat. Then she could see the wave of confusion pass over his eyes, "No, my father said they stole the heart of the island, he said—"

"He probably felt guilty! And I'm sure he didn't feel good about whelping a psychopath either!" She laughed, knowing she was poking the bear, part of her wanting to.

He looked at her again and the rage and heat returned. "You know nothing, you bitch!" And his fight was renewed, their bodies a writhing, kicking, biting mass of limbs, until she slammed into the beach on her back, the dull *thud* echoing through her body. Then she looked up and realized he was holding a shiny knife blade at her throat. It was short but looked very sharp.

He saw her looking at it and held it up with pride. "You like it? It's my obsidian scalpel from my pre-med days. It would have been so much more poetic to use your brother's switchblade, though it was rather . . . crude for me. But I had to sacrifice it to make my statement." He smiled. "Perhaps I'll get it back after all, once you're dead and I blame it on that guy." He pointed with the knife at a dead officer sprawled near the tree line—she couldn't help being relieved to see it wasn't Javier—the dark blood seeping into the sand like oil. "I'm sorry I won't get to take care of you in my preferred manner, but I'm kind of in a hurry today. However, I'm looking forward to taking care of that Lupe friend of yours, maybe even her uncle. Hell, maybe they'll make me police chief one day—"

A rush of adrenalin burst through Marisol's chest, radiating out to her limbs, her arms pulling free. He was so surprised and confused, he took his attention off the knife in his hand, and she hit his arm, sending the scalpel flying across the sand. She used the time to bash him on his ears, then in one swift move she grabbed him and rolled toward the water until she was over him and the surf was crashing against the side of his face. He sputtered as she held his neck down against the sand as he had done to her. There was something about seeing the hate-filled face gasping for breath that brought a joyous heat to her soul.

"I have just one more question for you before I push your tiny head under this wave for good. Why Lupe? What the hell did she do to you?"

He scoffed, spitting sea water all over her face. "That nosy gringa bitch! Her and her uncle were screwing it all up! I was going to get justice for all of us who are true Puerto Ricans in our hearts, not like her."

That was it. Something snapped, gave way in her head. Every fiber of her being wanted to hold his head beneath the waves. To watch him gasp for breath like a fish on a dock.

"Mari!"

The scream came from behind the resort, the sound of feet hitting packed dirt accompanying her name.

Then Lupe was careening to a stop in the sand, her uncle following, more officers gathering behind. Her friend looked just like she had in the vision Mari had when she was being strangled.

Even though she was sure he deserved to drown, she dropped Hernán's head and let it fall to the sand. She stood up, wiped the sand off her clothes, and said, "The bomb's in the most middle tube of the grandstand's scaffolding."

A group of officers rushed down and handcuffed Hernán, pulling him up and dragging him across the sand. The rest of them took off in the direction of the bandstand, as there was no time to radio and, given the sounds coming from the loudspeakers, the chaos had reached a fevered pitch.

Now they just had to make it in time before the murderer's bomb killed them all.

Chapter Thirty-two

Lupe

LUPE TOOK MARISOL by the arm and they ran. She was worried about her friend. Even in the shadows caused by the event lights, she could see finger-shaped bruises blooming across Marisol's throat, and her eyes looked . . . wild. Would she have drowned Hernán if they hadn't gotten there in time? Not that Lupe would have blamed her, but seeing her like that had given her a flashback to the summer before, when they'd fought while Javier was being attacked by El Cuco just a few feet away on the stage at Carlos's concert. The road to their friendship had been an unusual one—talk about odd couples—but one thing they both needed from each other was trust. Faith. And she had faith in Mari.

The group bunched up at the outskirts of the grandstand. The bomb squad was frantically working underneath the structure, and the people on top were completely panicked. The glowing ghost figures now surrounded the field and the crowd completely, as well as blocking the exit from the platform. They were just standing as if in vigil. Were they going to attack? Most of the people in the center seemed to think so, as they clung to one another, eyes wild with fright.

A microphone squawk broke through the white noise of panic, and the governor's voice was carrying over the crowd, temporarily dazing them.

"Everyone! Calm down! We must have order!"

"Order?" someone yelled. "Have you looked around? Easy for you to say up there!"

Then Sam's father, the developer, leaned over and barked into the microphone. "Easy for us to say! I just overheard an officer saying that the bomb squad is beneath us dismantling an incendiary device as we speak! We are at far more risk from the bomb than you are with the ghosts!"

"Bomb?!"

"He said there's a bomb here!"

"We have to get out of here!"

"Boy, what a complete idiot," Lupe said, mostly to herself.

"Ya think?" Marisol replied. She was still holding her head and weaving a bit. Lupe watched her out of the corner of her eye with concern.

"It wasn't a working bomb; besides, it's been dismantled," the chief said.

A person in the front cried out, "But what about the ghosts? Are they going to take our hearts?"

The sound of panic rose again, higher pitched this time, but people could only shuffle and push against one another as any possible escape route was blocked by the long dead who stood sentry, waiting for runners like a blue, glowing spiderweb.

The governor pulled the microphone away and tried to cover it, but they all could still hear him say, "That is not helpful, Michael!"

As if in a daze, Marisol started pushing through the police and first responders, then around them, and toward the stand. Lupe tried to catch her by the sleeve but missed, and hurried to catch up. "What are you doing?"

Marisol yanked a stack of papers from her backpack and began to climb the side of the structure.

What was she doing? Was her head injury worse than she let on?

Lupe and Javier followed closely behind, until all three stood on the same level as the mucky-mucks at their tableclothed dais.

It was the first time she had gotten a good look at the group at the dais, the investors and politicians. They were as she expected, doughy gray-haired white men with expensive suits, impatient expressions, and beautiful wives at their sides. One of the women, the proof that you could indeed be too rich and too thin, was sitting as if she were afraid to touch anything, her face like someone had pulled on her perfectly coiffed chignon and tightened her skin. These were the people deciding the future of the island?

While the governor was still distracted by Sam's father, Marisol grabbed the mic, waved the papers, and addressed the crowd.

"My fellow Boricuas! Are you going to let these men, these greedy swindlers, take our island?" She gestured around to the people sitting and standing on the platform, their pale faces reddening with rage. She turned back to face them, pulling the mic in closer, thwarting a bald-headed man who was trying to reach around and take it from her. "I have here a petition signed by over a thousand island residents, protesting the sale of our precious resources in our time of great vulnerability for the profit of U.S. corporations! A sale perpetrated by one of our very own!" She shook the stack of paper at the governor.

Lupe watched the crowd and saw fear being replaced by anger.

Wow, Marisol was good at this.

"This resort"—she indicated the oversize building behind her—"was built on protected land, land that should belong to the people of—"

The governor lurched across his coconspirators then and yanked the microphone from Marisol's hand. "That's enough, you little bitch!" Realizing his tone was untoward, he turned and addressed the crowd once more with the confidence of someone who was rarely questioned. "I'm sure this little girl has her heart in right place—"

Lupe groaned. The man couldn't have made a worse choice of words and it seemed most of the crowd knew it.

Marisol leaned closer and yelled, "They're also trying to privatize all of Puerto Rico's beaches!" She indicated the crowd. "Our beaches!"

The mumbling of the crowd elevated to yelling, anger growing.

The governor plastered on his biggest smile. "I assure you, this is total fantasy. Now—"

Then another voice cut in from behind the man, and Lupe saw Sam, who had just climbed up the other side of the platform—the ghosts let him through!—and was moving toward the governor and his father, with Esteban close behind him.

His mouth was moving, but in the chaos of the moment the words were lost. When he reached his father, he said into the microphone, "No, it's not made up, and I have proof!"

Sam's father moved forward. "Sam! Get off the stage! You have no place here either!"

"Actually, Dad, I do have a place here. And so does she." He pointed to Marisol. "What she said is right. You bribed and lied and took land that didn't belong to you. And now we believe"—he indicated Lupe, Marisol, and Javier—"that these spirits are here to take back what is theirs." The heads in the crowd turned toward the ghosts that surrounded them.

His father looked incredulous. "What? This is not our doing! Lord only knows what local heathen rituals have brought forth—"

"No. *You* did this, Dad. You all did." He pointed to the other people on the dais. "And now you're going to fix it."

They all scoffed and harrumphed and turned to each other. His father then stepped up to act as a spokesman for the greedy bunch. "And how do you kids propose we do that?"

Marisol answered in a clear, forceful voice, "You need to abandon this project, donate the land, and return it to protected status."

The investors on the stage laughed then. Actually laughed. Several of them had begun gathering their things and preparing to leave when a dozen ghosts appeared behind them, their hands reaching forward, grabbing the edges of the men's suits, pulling on them with bony fingers, reaching toward their chests. Screams rose from the crowd and Lupe saw the ghosts weaving their way among the people, their moaning high-pitched like a buzzing she could feel in her teeth, and people in the audience began to climb over each other in panic.

Sam's father pointed to Esteban and shouted, "You! You created this special-effect light show." He pointed wildly at the ghosts all around them. "And you killed people and took their hearts just to shut down this project!"

One of the other officers pulled Hernán, who was still hand-cuffed, in front of the grandstand, the crowd parting for them.

Esteban's voice boomed from behind. Tío didn't need a mic. "No, the murders were done by this young man." He pointed to the front of the stage and at the younger Torres. "And he even planted a badly made bomb right beneath this very grandstand in an attempt to kill all of you here." A gasp from the crowd, as if a stagehand were holding a sign with directions. "But these kids caught him." He indicated Lupe, Javier, Marisol, and Sam.

Emboldened, Sam stepped up, grabbed the microphone, and held up a USB thumb drive. "This contains emails from my father's investing group implicating"—he gestured around at the group of men—"these people, and ironically initiated by one of the men whose son was killed in the bay, outlining pay-offs and building shortcuts. And about the next stage when they planned to control access to all the beaches on the main island and this one."

Sam had barely got out the last word when his father stepped up, arrogance exaggerating his movements, grabbed the drive from his hand, dropped it to the dais floor, and smashed it beneath his heel. Then he said to Esteban, "Clearly, my son doesn't understand how these things work." Smugness spread on his lips like oil.

Lupe's uncle stepped forward and stood beside Sam. "That's okay, Señor. You see, your son emailed all those files to my department moments ago." He nodded his head and a group of officers came up onto the dais and surrounded the investors. "Seems we have all the proof we need."

Marisol broke in. "Clearly, *you* don't understand how this works!"

Lupe felt like shouting *Can I get an amen?*

The governor straightened his jacket. "So, that young man was the murderer? The one pulling the hearts out of people?"

Dávila glared at him. "It would seem that way."

"Well then, the true threat is over, is it not?"

Chapter Thirty-three

Marisol

MARISOL'S PHONE RANG surprisingly loudly in the hush of the crowd. It was Carlos. Shit! Carlos was across the field in the neighboring concert venue, and didn't even know what was going on! She had to tell him all was okay!

"Carlos! We caught him! And the bomb—"

"Mari, it's not over."

She glanced over at Lupe and Esteban, who were looking at her with concern. Something about this felt off. "But it is! They dismantled—"

"Stop talking and listen to me." She gestured for Esteban and Lupe to come closer, and she put her phone on Speaker.

"We were having trouble with the power, we tracked it down, and my electrician found out it was rerouted."

Esteban stepped forward. "Rerouted to where?" He waved for one of the officers to come closer for the order sure to come.

"Chief, is the grandstand on a metal plate of some kind?"

The officer jumped off the side of the platform and kicked aside the squares of sod that covered the ground. He looked up and nodded to the chief.

"Yes."

Everyone was quiet then, ghosts and humans.

A muffled voice on the other end of the phone.

"My electrician says to look along the edges, see if there's something clipped to them."

Several officers joined the first, and they scrambled around, pulling up the squares of grass and tossing them in the air. And then, even from the grandstand, Marisol could see dozens of cables clipped to the end of the metal sheet that ran beneath the metal grandstand.

Esteban looked down at Hernán, standing directly in front of the dais on the ground, flanked by two officers. Marisol followed his gaze and saw Hernán raising his handcuffed hands, and looking at his watch with a smile.

The chief bellowed, "Get everyone off the grandstand! Now!"

Marisol stumbled toward the edge, Lupe and Javier on either side of her, but before they could get over the edge, a huge flash lit up the night, and in one stretched and terrifying second the metal bandstand beneath and below them glowed and crackled like the ghosts, arcs of electricity reaching up into the night like reverse lightning.

Marisol could hear Carlos's scream from the phone in her hands and echoing from the speakers on the stage across the way, his complete terror mirroring her own as everyone they truly cared for lit up like flares.

Chapter Thirty-four

Javier

IT MUST HAVE lasted only a few seconds—electricity worked like that—but it felt like a year of Javier's life was zapped from his body in a frizzle of light.

It came with a sound first, a buzzing accompanied by his best friend's amplified screams, followed by a series of sparks.

Then the smell, metallic and sulfurous.

Then the light. They all lit up. Lit as if glowing from within. Javier felt it in every nerve ending, at the end of every hair follicle, and on the surface of his eyeballs. He knew he was going to die. He'd done the hard work, gotten clean, but he was still going to die young. He closed his eyes and began to pray.

And then it was pulled out of him in a rush, and the ghosts around the platform were glowing even brighter, their faces lifted to the heavens, the electricity going through them and then arcing into the night sky.

And then it was over.

Just . . . over.

As if it never happened.

But there was no denying the whiff of ozone hanging in the

air and the look on everyone's faces on the grandstand. They had all felt it, experienced it. Javier wondered if he had a streak of gray in his hair after that.

The crowd had been completely silent after the incident, but slowly they came back to themselves, incredulous, questioning what they saw, unbelieving.

Esteban Dávila kneeled down at the front of the platform and yanked Hernán by the shirt, pulling him up to the edge. "So, the bomb was a decoy?" Fury made his voice even gruffer than usual, and Javier wondered if he was going to kill the younger officer right then and there. Not sure he would blame him either.

Hernán scoffed, seemingly uncaring of the huge man's anger. "I don't have a clue how to make a bomb. I just heard something once about lawn fertilizer and a timing device. They use cell phones as triggers in the movies." He laughed. "But it bought some time, didn't it? Now, electricity, that I know something about."

He was proud of himself. The psychopath was proud.

Dávila threw him back and onto the ground. "Get this trash out of here!" he yelled to the officers below.

Lupe shook her fist, yelling after Torres, "And I would have succeeded, too, if it weren't for those pesky kids!"

Javier just stared at her.

She smiled and shrugged. *"Scooby-Doo."*

"Meddling," he said.

"What?"

"If it weren't for you meddling kids."

She smiled at him.

He fought back a return smile. "Well, it's not as if we don't have cartoon reruns here in Puerto Rico. It's not the moon, you know!"

Then she turned around and faced the collection of clueless investors. "Well, it seems these ghosts have saved your asses,"

Lupe said to the group. They looked even paler than usual. That was his girl! Talking smack moments after almost getting electrocuted.

"But why aren't they going away?" Sam's father's agitation seemed to rise. "Why are these . . . beings here? Why punish me?"

Javier scoffed. *Of course, he thinks it's all about him.* But then a figure came forward in the crowd, moving almost in slow motion. The crowd parted to let an old man through. He stopped when he arrived in front of the grandstand, standing where Hernán had been. Javier recognized Chachu, the old man he and Lupe had met in the forest, who'd given them a ride after they'd seen the ghosts on the beach.

He had a surprisingly strong voice for an old man. He yelled up toward the stage. "Because they were protecting the land, not your greedy little lives."

Sam's father scoffed. "But why now? I'm not the first developer to purchase land when it's cheap!"

Marisol replied with wonder in her voice, as if with each word another piece of the puzzle clicked in. "No, but you're the first since the last category-five hurricane."

The governor spoke next. "What? What are you talking about? Why don't you leave this situation to the grown-ups, querida." The last word, usually a term of endearment, was dripping with condescension and judgment. Clearly the man had no idea with whom he was dealing.

Javier was shocked that Marisol did not give the man her laser gaze, but instead her eyes lit up with understanding. "Three hundred and twelve people who were killed by San Felipe Segundo of 1928. Some of those were from right here on Vieques."

Esteban Dávila chimed in as understanding spread to him. "Yes, my grandfather often spoke of it. The sugarcane industry on Vieques was destroyed; it took more than ten years for the island to recover. It was never the same."

Chachu nodded. "That was when the U.S. Navy came in and seized large sections of the island, including the defunct sugar plantation."

"It was Hernán's great-grandfather who brokered that seizure!" Marisol said.

"They dug up the graveyard over there when building a munitions building!" Javier yelled. "They dug up the bones of all the locals killed in the 1928 hurricane and left them on a garbage heap!"

The crowd gasped and growled with disapproval.

"That's when the spirits first visited." Chachu said, seemingly putting together puzzles of information of his own. "Those who were killed in the 1928 hurricane." Everyone looked around into the faces of the ghostly visages all around them.

"But . . . those people were killed all over the island, not just people from here. Why are there so many?" Javier looked around at the hundreds of beings surrounding them.

"I don't know, joven." Chachu's voice sounded tired. Javier didn't blame him. He was tired, too. "But those who died that day are here."

Lupe's voice cut in as she leaned into the mic, not with a challenging tone but a curious one. "But how can you know that?"

Chachu smiled sadly. "Because my grandmother is among them. She was killed when the roof flew off her house. That house that you visited near the beach. She came back that time before, too, before the navy left." He pointed up to the dais. "And now she's standing right beside you."

Lupe spun around and looked into the face of an old woman with strips of gray hair pulled into a messy bun on the back of her head. Her clothes were in rags, but she stood with a confidence that seemed to say she belonged there. That

these were her people. Javier could tell the woman was smiling. After a moment's hesitation Lupe stepped forward, nodded to the ghost woman, and said, "Hello, Abuela."

"And now they arise to protect the sacred land. To keep it
from happening again."

The group on the dais all turned to look at Sam's father
and the investors. Esteban Dávila spoke into the microphone
that the governor still clutched. "And punish those who would
profit from it."

The faces of the doughy investors went pale as their terrified
eyes locked with the crowd, then with the empty eye sockets of
the ghosts that surrounded them. A low humming noise began
to come from the spirits, rising above their heads, into the air
above the clearing, rising in volume and strength until it was
an almost stereotypical ghost or zombie moan. But as desensi-
tized as they all were, hearing this sound in real life, mere feet
away, was mind-blowingly terrifying. Javier felt all the heat
leave his body and the hairs on his arms and legs stand up, and
he wondered if they were all going to be made to pay for that
group's greed after all.

The sound was rising and rising, to almost unbearable lev-
els. Could a sound kill them? As Javier covered his ears with
his hands, he began to think it could.

Sam's father cowered behind Chief Dávila and screamed.
"All right! All right! We'll return the land!" The words rang
over the crowd like the peal of bells.

Esteban Dávila, his voice as cool as a mountaintop spring,
broke through the silence so clearly it could be heard across
the entire property. "Does your group of investors agree?"

The men were nodding their heads in unison like kinder-
garteners caught with stolen crayons.

"Well, you have many witnesses." The chief turned to the
governor with a look that held an entire conversation. Javier
could see that not only did Dávila know of the governor's

intention of replacing him, but he also knew that there was no way he could do it now. "I assume you will make sure the proper paperwork is filed, Señor Gobernador?"

"N-Now, look here. This installation has a substantial dollar value attached to it," the governor stammered.

"Well you can bill *him*," Sam said, pointing to his own father.

The sounds of the ghosts on the podium began to rise again, and the abuela reached for the governor. He looked over with terror, cleared his throat, and spoke into the forgotten microphone in his hand. "Of course. Seguro. My people will take care of it first thing tomorrow."

"Tonight," Dávila ordered, the one word holding as much weight as the dais beneath them.

The politician hesitated for an instant, not accustomed to taking orders from anyone other than rich investors, but clearly unable to back down. His shoulders dropped and he nodded. "Yes, tonight."

Javier stepped forward. "And return these poor people to their graves with the honor they deserve. And leave them in peace."

The governor bowed his head. "Yes."

In that instant it was as if the air had been removed from around the group on the dais, just sucked out, Lupe and Marisol's hair rising as if with a gust of wind, and then the spirits on the platform just . . . disappeared from the platform as if they were never there. They all looked out toward the crowd and saw the spirits regathering there, then dispersing outward like the glowing waves of the bio bay, moving slowly back into the trees, back to wherever they had awoken from.

And they were gone.

Then it was as if everyone stirred from a deep sleep. Conversation rose, people cried and embraced, and music began playing from the nearby concert stage in celebration.

Sam's father and the other investors were escorted off the property, Sam's father in handcuffs.

The governor was quietly scurrying off the other side when Lupe's uncle grabbed his coat sleeve. "Don't think you're getting off free, Gobernador. We'll be watching you." The weaselly politician yanked his arm away and almost fell off the edge of the dais, his thick, black eyebrows raised. Then he scuttled off the edge and was gone, his cronies surrounding him in a wave.

The crowd began to move en masse toward the concert music, and Javier was excited to hear a voice announce that his friend Carlos's concert would begin soon.

As they walked, Lupe smiled at him and bumped her hip against his in a playful way. He paused, then put his arm around her shoulders, and they walked as they had for most of the last summer. Honestly, he kind of needed the support. His head was still throbbing from the whack he'd taken on the back of the head.

But they didn't get far.

"Where do you children think you're going?" Esteban called from behind them.

They turned back and saw him pointing to an ambulance and EMT staff, who had driven up behind the grandstand.

"We're fine, Tío!" Lupe said in an exasperated tone.

Marisol limped up from behind. "Speak for yourself, Blondie. I got the shit kicked out of me by a serial killer. Then electrocuted."

Lupe smiled as she turned them around. "Whine, whine, whine." But she put her arm around Mari and they walked back together.

Chapter Thirty-five

Marisol

THE EMERGENCY MEDICAL techs checked them all out after the electrocution attempt, but it seemed the ghosts had buffered it all. Marisol wasn't surprised. Though the techs gave her a hard time about her injuries from the fight, in the end they had to concede that it was just a lot of bruising and cuts. They gave her ibuprofen and treated her cuts, and she promised to see her doctor the next day. The group of friends started making their way to the performance area to support Carlos and his concert.

It was one of those times when Marisol felt like a mutant third wheel on a bicycle built for two, which happened often when she was with Lupe and Javier. There had still been tension between them when she arrived on the island, but a near-death experience with bombs, electrocution, and the supernatural tended to smooth rough edges. Still, it was hard to share her friend and watch them walking with their arms around each other. But then Lupe paused and looked back. She reached for Marisol with a smile and pulled her forward with her other arm until she was part and parcel of the arm-in-arm walking. These people had a family feel, good and bad. She'd enjoyed the volunteering the last few months, even hung out with some of the other volunteers, but Lupe was the first close friend she'd had in a very long time. Even Javier. He was whiny, but he had a good heart.

And speaking of friends, Marisol was going to make sure to head back to Yabucoa and assure Abuelita that her grandmother was no longer angry, that she was at peace once again.

Sam led them to the back way toward the stage access, and when they walked up Marisol was certain they would be turned away. When she saw bouncers like this at clubs in San Juan, they normally took one look at her and could tell she was a broke-ass nobody and sent her to wait at the end of the three-mile line. But Sam flashed his smile and a laminated pass that hung around his neck, and they were immediately let through.

As they were walking up the stage steps, a thin girl with big blond hair and way over-collagened lips came rushing down, pushing by them.

"That's the last time I let the network ship me out to work on some Latin diva's makeup!"

Marisol watched her scurry away on her platform Louboutins. "Um, Carlos is many things, but I don't think a diva is one of them."

Lupe chuckled. "This I gotta see!"

When they reached backstage, Carlos was standing in front of a lit mirror, pulling tissues away from his neck.

Marisol smiled at his reflection. "You starting to believe your own press, Papi Gringo?"

"What you talkin' 'bout, Mari?" he replied into the mirror.

"We just saw your makeup artist storming away talking about what a diva you are."

Carlos scoffed. "*Artist*? In her dreams! Man, they send these people from the networks and they try to whitewash me! That woman tried to use pancake three shades paler than my skin." He framed his face with his hands in a Vogue pose. "Why mess with perfection?" As his face broke into his chart-topping smile, Marisol couldn't help laughing.

"We need you on stage, jefe!" A woman with headphones and a clipboard scooted Carlos to the stage, and as he got closer to the glow of the lights, he slowly transformed into Papi Gringo. When a tech shoved a microphone into his hand, the transformation was complete. He strutted onto the stage and a huge wave of sound rose and crested over them as the audience welcomed him.

All these people, all this security, just for little annoying Carlos who she dated for fifteen minutes in seventh grade. She couldn't help but grin big. He annoyed the shit out of her, but even she had to admit that her childhood friend had become a big deal.

But tonight, he wasn't Carlos, he was in his full Papi Gringo glory.

Papi Gringo was strutting across the stage, microphone in hand, oversized gold chain gleaming and swinging, swinging and gleaming. She listened closely, something she never used to do, as she would always end up massively disappointed by the ridiculous lyrics. The song was about dark winds, falling skies, loss of control. His new music actually said something that mattered, that made you feel something, unlike his early work that was pretty much the objectification of women set to a beat. Reggaeton could be misogynistic, and she believed that Carlos was better than that.

The four of them, Sam, Javier, Lupe, and Marisol, stood side by side in the backstage of the open-air arena, the noise of the crowd louder with the evening's excitement. Though she preferred a quiet plena, it was impossible for Marisol to not get pulled into the energy of the music, the driving beat and shouted poetry. Sam appeared in front of her, hips moving, and took one of her hands. She laughed; she couldn't help it. "Oh, rich white boy gonna dance?" Then he pulled her into a tight hold in one fluid move, his hips smoothly shifting left to right, his feet nimble and moving with the beat. He was grinding his hips against hers in a very stealth reggaeton move. She turned to Lupe. "Hey, even I gotta admit that pretty white boy got some moves!" They danced for the rest of the song, and everything else fell away. How long had it been since she'd danced? Really danced? She felt it in the core of her body, the movements second nature, the beat matching the pulse of her blood. During a spin she caught Carlos glancing at them as he performed, smiling that one-sided grin of his, Lupe and Javier clapping along behind them. That was when it really hit Marisol.

She was part of something.

Actually part of it, not on the outside looking in with a scowl.

She wasn't sure what to even do with that!

The song ended, and Sam brought her hand to his mouth, and pressed his soft lips on the back of her hand in a feather kiss. Lord, she didn't know entitled boys could be so thoughtful!

Carlos's voice echoed over the crowd like a god's. "For this next song I want to bring up El Trovador de Isla Nena, Vieques' own, Mon Silva!" An older man, white-haired but handsome in a white suit and hat, made his way to a stool that was placed in the center of the stage. Before he sat down, he tipped his hat and bowed to the audience. Then he sat with his acoustic guitar and a big smile. Carlos bowed and ran offstage to give the local singer the spotlight.

He was out of breath, but Carlos turned to them with a smile. "Saw this guy at a party in town during the holidays. He's amazing. He sings a song about David Sanes Rodriguez and his death. The local who was killed during the navy exercises on the island."

Carlos turned back, and called them all together until they were in a backstage huddle, the soothing guitar music and melodic vocals the perfect background.

Carlos put his arms around Javier and Lupe and smiled at Sam. "I've been wanting to share this with you for a long time." He locked eyes with Javier, and Marisol could see the shame in Javier's eyes for blowing his friend off for so long. "But, honestly, I was afraid of how you might react."

"Man, you can tell me anything, you know that," Javier scoffed.

Carlos looked serious. Marisol wasn't sure she'd ever seen him look so serious. What did he have to say?

"Not this. Not until now. Plus, I was worried if it got out it would mean the end of my career, my friendships. But after another summer where we faced death together, I've realized that life is too short, and you never know when it will come crashing . . . or exploding, to an end. And I want to be true to myself. And to those I love."

Carlos stared into his eyes. "Javi, man, you're my best friend. I should have told you this years ago."

Javier put his hands out in impatience. "What, hermano?"

He swallowed and said, "I'm gay."

Marisol just stood there and stared at him. So that was the missing piece to the puzzle that was Carlos? But her eyes moved to Javier. That was where the show was.

Javier stared for a minute, his eyes intense. Everyone seemed to be holding their breath, wondering if he'd stalk away in one of his tantrums. Then a slow smile spread across his face and he stepped up to Carlos and said, "Thanks for trusting us with the truth, 'mano!" And he hugged him tight.

Carlos pulled back and looked in his face. "So we're cool?"

Javier's eyes softened. "Why wouldn't we be? You're the closest thing to a brother I've ever had, Carlos. I want you to be happy, and yourself."

Carlos looked over at Lupe and Marisol.

Lupe stepped closer, pulled Carlos's head close to hers, and planted a wet, sloppy kiss on his cheek.

He turned to Marisol with a weird look. Ah yes, that awkward two weeks of dating when they were kids. He couldn't possibly think that mattered now, could he?

"Mari?"

She let him suffer for a moment, then a smile teased up her lips. "And I thought you couldn't maintain a relationship because you were a superficial prick."

Carlos smiled back. "Well, I still might be that. But I have been in a relationship."

Then he walked over to Sam and kissed him right on the lips, and Sam kissed him back.

Aha! That makes total sense.

When they finally broke apart, Lupe indicated between them. "So, how long has this been going on?"

Sam smiled shyly, Carlos's arm draped over his shoulders. "A few months. We met at a concert in Old San Juan and have been together ever since."

Carlos turned to Javier. "Why do you think I did this concert for those assholes?" He indicated the direction of the grandstand. He looked in Sam's ocean-blue eyes. "I did it for him."

Mon Silva's song came to an end, the last notes of the guitar hanging in the air like a scent. It was silent for a moment, then the crowd started stamping their feet and clapping in syncopation, louder and louder until it became its own music, the beats resounding through their feet, up into their bellies, and shook their hearts.

Mon Silva motioned Carlos back onstage; they were going to do a song together.

Carlos put his hands together and bowed to his friends. He looked different. His face was electric, glowing out from his pores. "Well, if you'll excuse me, my dear friends: the show must go on."

Marisol nodded toward the stage and the audience. "Are you going to tell them?"

Carlos sighed. "Maybe someday. I don't know. For right now, it means everything that you guys know."

Then he strutted on to the stage, clapping above his head, the crowd roaring when they saw him. He brought the mic to his face and Papi Gringo was back, but Marisol realized that though he hadn't come out publicly, his stage personality had changed forever. He'd already begun with his latest album: songs about things that mattered to the island.

The voices of Carlos and Mon Silva blended like aged Barrilito rum and sparkly soda, the poetic words of his ballad about the island of Vieques rising, up and over the trees. And it was their island once again. Their identity and hearts were not for sale or barter.

She had to imagine that the spirits were not only appeased, but pleased.

Chapter Thirty-six

Lupe

THEY RODE TOGETHER back to the mainland the next day. Carlos had his own chartered ferry, so there was lots of room for the group of friends. Lupe looked at him sitting next to Sam, so totally himself in this group, people he could actually trust, and she admired Carlos for having the courage to truly be himself, not what his audience or his managers or anyone else expected him to be.

At least he knew.

She was only just starting to figure out who she was, but it was her uncle who provided the steady foundation on which she was building. And now she didn't have to worry about him losing his job. Well, at least for today. With the political climate on the island, post-hurricane, it was hard to tell where it was all going to go. Or if there would even be anyone left on the island to lead. But for now, her uncle was employed. After all, it wasn't just a job for him, it was his identity.

Javier walked up to her, held her by the upper arms, and kissed her forehead. It was so tender, so sweet, it was hard to justify the icy feeling in her belly. The way he held her arms reminded her of the argument they had had the first day she came to Vieques. It wasn't that he was angry; it was that he had taken it out on her. And it had continued throughout the last few days, in different ways. He was distant. She understood trauma, it was something she dealt with every week in counseling, but she also knew facing it didn't make for a good time for romance.

He pulled back and looked into her eyes, as if he could see her thoughts. "Lupe. We okay?"

She didn't lie, wouldn't lie, particularly not to him. "We're okay, just . . . not the same. Is that okay?" She hated the tip up on the end of her words, the slight asking-for-permission tone. But these were new waters she was navigating.

"I guess it's going to have to be." His gaze moved off, but he stayed next to her. She was about to ask him if he was okay when he started talking. "I think I have some things to work out. The hurricane, the poor people left without power, the paper towel–throwing president. I don't know what to do with all this anger." He looked back into her face. "But I do know I don't want to take it out on you." He moved a strand of hair out of her eyes, his thick, calloused fingers amazingly gentle, his brown eyes soft. "You're the last one I want to take it out on."

She looked at him for a second, then stepped on tiptoe and placed her lips gently against his, the salted wind blowing her hair around them in a cloud, the boat rocking and swaying them with it. "I know you'll work it out, Javier. You just need some time and space. But I'll be here when you're ready."

His eyes got glassy. "Does this mean we won't see each other again this summer?"

She looked at him sideways. "What are you talking about, Utierre? Aren't we friends? Isn't this our gang? Hmm . . . five friends again." She pulled in Marisol and Carlos and Sam until they were standing in a mass like a human tree trunk. "Cangrejos, the sequel."

He shook his head. "No. Too much baggage with that name. We need a new name for this new configuration."

Marisol offered, "The Ghostbusters? I get to be Holtzmann!"

Carlos shook his head. "No, Javi's right, it has to be something new."

It came to Lupe in a flash. "Los corazones."

Groans from all around.

Carlos said with a smirk, "What, finding a human heart in your bag made you think it was a good name for our little group?"

"No, hear me out. He tried to take the hearts out of people here, because he felt they were taking the heart of the island. But it's our hearts that cracked this thing wide open *and* thwarted him."

"Thwarted, huh?" Javier was smiling.

Marisol shrugged. "Sure, why not? To los corazones."

She stretched her hand out in the middle of the group, and one by one they put their hands together in the center like the hub of a wheel, skin colors of different shades, and shook them up and down, then pulled back with a flourish, giggling like they were five years old again.

Lupe wished she'd known them all since she was five. How would things be now if she'd had friends like this her whole life? People to laugh with, fight with. She was just glad she had them now.

They walked off the ferry together, like some sort of superhero group, but when they reached the line of cars it hit her that they would all be going in different directions. Sam and Carlos, in the limo to his next show. Javier, home to find new work since the resort was closing.

As they were saying goodbye, Javier stopped. "Wait, where

are you two going?" he asked Lupe and Marisol. They smiled
at each other, then back at Javier.

"Well, it seems Lupe here has never had a proper Puerto
Rican teenage vacation."

He raised his eyebrows. "Oh no? And what does that en-
tail?"

Lupe added, "Well, my uncle has a condo at Luquillo that
he's loaning us for a few days."

"Yeah, we're going to lie on the beach, soak up the sun,
read books, drink something touristy and frozen."

"Touristy, huh?"

Marisol added, "Yeah, Luquillo Beach isn't totally recovered but the sand and water are still there and maybe, when
our eyes aren't closed under our sunglasses, we'll check out
some boys on the beach."

Lupe slapped her arm. "You can do that. I'm just out for the
relaxation piece. Not even sure what that feels like."

Javier was quiet, looking at Lupe with a sad smile. "I think
that sounds perfect. You deserve to finally have a real vacation, Miss Lupe." He gave her a warm, all-enveloping hug, and
another kiss on the forehead. "No pedicures, though?"

Lupe rolled her eyes. "No way! I've always wanted to hike
in El Yunque. Though I hear it's pretty beat up."

Marisol nodded. "Yeah, the public areas are closed, probably will be for a while, but I know this guide in Cubuy who
can take us the back way, from Naguabo. It'll still be rough,
but I'd like to see how nature is coming back."

"Yeah, you'd be surprised how quickly the plant life recov-
ers," Javier added. "See you next week?"

"Damn straight, Utierre."

Javier raised his eyebrows. "That sounded a little too much
like the chief."

Lupe blew him a kiss, and they started making their way

past the ferry parking lot and toward Marisol's car in the distance.

As they walked, Marisol perked up. "Oh! There are some fascinating plant species in El Yunque I'd love to classify! I haven't had time this past semester, what with the hurricane recovery."

Lupe held up her hand. "Wait, wait. No classifications, no research into local folklore, no Chupacabra hunting. Just . . . hiking. Muddy boots, warm bottled water, granola bars, and a view of the entire island at the top."

Marisol smiled and nodded. "Okay."

They walked to Marisol's car in comfortable silence, listening to the chug of the next ferry pulling away from the dock.

Marisol stopped. "Wait!"

"What?"

"Are you sure you're not up for some Chupacabra hunting?"

Lupe kept walking. "No."

"Oh c'mon! And there's a special monster that's talked about in Luquillo . . . what's its name . . . ?"

Acknowledgments

As always, thanks to my fabulous agent and amiga, Linda Camacho. She keeps me sane. Well, relatively. (She's not a miracle worker!) And my brilliant editor, Ali Fisher. She saw the potential in this story and these characters from the beginning, and I consider her the midwife to Marisol. Thank you both for your incredible faith and support.

To the Tor Teen publicity team. When I did the acknowledgments for the first book, I didn't know them yet. But I would come to think of them as superheroes. Particular thanks to Saraciea Fennell, Isa Caban, Zakiya Jamal, and Anthony Parisi. You SO rock, thank you! And the director of production for Macmillan Audio, Guy Oldfield, and the brilliant Almarie Guerra for bringing these stories to life in the audiobooks.

Muchísimas gracias to Adriana M. Martinez Figueroa for the incredibly thoughtful and detailed sensitivity read. She is a true scholar, and I look forward to watching her career blossom.

As always, thanks to my Vermont College of Fine Arts family. Particularly Cori McCarthy and Amy Rose Capetta, for sage counsel, support, and lots of laughter.

Muchas gracias to Las Musas, a group of amazing Latinx writers who support and cheer each other through this wild writing life. Thank you for making me feel part of things, part of una familia. I'm honored to be a member.

To the Speculative Literature Foundation, for the grant that helped fund the research trip for this novel.

Thank you to my cousin Tere Dávila, for parallel writing with me in Napa while I powered through the first draft. My tío Esteban, for giving me a home to work from in Luquillo, where this book was formed, and for inspiring my favorite character. My husband, Doug, who grounds me and supports all my work. My son, Carlos, who is my creative twin in so many ways, and my inspiration.

The biggest thank-you for this book goes to my brother, George Hagman. While supporting me with revisions to *Five Midnights,* he was the one who suggested another book with this group of characters. "What about zombies on Vieques!" Though they turned out to be more ghosts than zombies, this story would never have happened without his help, support, and brilliant mind.

And thank you to the island of Puerto Rico and its people for continuing to inspire me. A portion of my advance for this book will be going to post-Maria work that is still going on.

And thank YOU, dear reader!